Dark Confessions

Dark Confessions
By
Fritz O'Skennick

Cover Photography
By
Adam Foreman

Cover Art Photo Manipulation
By
Jayde Antonin

Dedicated to Shaun & Romana

With a big thank you to Adam Foreman &
Jayde Antonin for all their time and hard
work on the cover art of this book…
I really appreciate it guys… x

Also, thank you to Allpoetry.com for
banning the first 2 parts of this story as
being too graphic and not in accordance
with site regulations as your censorship of
my work fired me up and inspired me to
complete this tale and further explore the
potential depths and passions of this
Character…

Thank you…

Contents

Foreword

"Dark Confessions" is an intense new novella told in the unique style of dark writer **'Fritz O'Skennick'** and concentrates on the darker nature of man, exploring the facets and mind states of murder, revenge and the lengths we'd go to in the name of love, honor and redemption...

It follows the story of Reggie, a scrap yard owner with a dark secret… Following the continual harassment of a gang that loiter on the abandoned industrial estate where Reggie lives and trades scrap, a break in results in the accidental murder of a gang member. Horrified by the potential consequences that could follow, he is forced to creatively and efficiently dispose of the body.

This is quickly followed by a night of carnage and revenge that forces him to evaluate his nature and the dark impulses that grow within him, justified only in that his victims are those that have wronged him.

He then meets and falls in love with Tess, quickly realizing that she is more like him than either would like to admit.

And so in the betrayal of friends, the death of a mobster, a case containing a million in cash with the mob hot on their trail to retrieve it, they are forced to embrace their natures in a fight for their lives with devastating consequences in an explosive finale of love, vengeance and death…

Fritz O'Skennick is an accomplished creative artist and writer with many strings to his bow. As a singer/songwriter, novelist, playwright/actor & performance poet, he has enjoyed varying successes with a number of his projects.

Previously published, some of his lighter work has appeared in various anthologies with other poets as produced by United Press.

His solo debut into literary publication was **"Touching the Darkness"** a highly anticipated anthology of his dark poetry that concentrates solely on his darker work that many have come to enjoy via Allpoetry.com and via performances throughout Wales and parts of England.

His second book **"Fear the Reaper"** is a unique, intense, first-person psychological crime thriller that tells a schizophrenic tale of love, loss, revenge and madness.

This was quickly followed by his third book **"The Darkness Verses The Light"** which is a mixed genre collection of poetry, prose and short stories.

His fourth book **"Who is John Doe?"** is a unique supernatural drama based on his popular stage show of the same name.

His fifth book **"Of Darkness and Light"** is a collection of poetry and prose, featuring new work and also many outstanding collaborative works with fellow poets from all over the World, including a collaboration that features no less than 40 poets in 1 poem as orchestrated and edited by Fritz.

His debut album **"UNspokeN"** (music) was released on Petrified Records in 2005 amidst a string of impressive reviews and radio play all over the world.

Playwright and acting credits include **"It could Happen to You"** and **"Who is John Doe?"** as produced by the former theatre company "Progress Cymru".

He is presently working on a second album of his music **"UNbrokeN",** his new book **"Just the Lyrics"** and writing his new series of sci-fi books **"Temporal Medium"**.

For further details of his poetry go to
http://allpoetry.com/Fritz%20O%20skennick

For further details of his music go to
http://www.myspace.com/fracturedpersona

For further details of his performance poetry go to
http://www.myspace.com/fritzo39skennick

Dark Confessions
...In the beginning...

Where do I begin?

Probably be best to tell you a bit about myself, I suppose...
My name is Reggie and I own a scrap-yard that adjoins an
abandoned industrial estate. I've always got by in my trade,
people pay me to take their crappy old cars, appliances,
computers, TVs, etc, others pay me to cannibalize them for
spare parts. An amicable arrangement that suits everyone
involved and if I make a bit of extra cash in the meantime,
then all the better... Life was sweet...

I'm a simple man with simple needs and those needs were
met, I wanted for nothing. I'd even built a garden area
behind the yard, fenced off, unseen and unknown to the
world. It gave me pleasure; it made me so proud that I
could create something so beautiful in a place as desolate as
this... Even had two Alsatians, Jerry and Trixie, they were
house dogs but they also made for a good deterrent to
anyone thinking of breaking in and nobody ever did... My
life was ideal...

Until one day, a gang of kids... Now I say a gang, I'm not
really sure what constitutes a gang to be honest... There
were actually four of them, late teens/early twenties in age,
started hanging around. I could tell they were trouble from
the off. Sitting around, drinking beers, shooting up, yep,
they were trouble alright. Not worth the flesh they were
printed on, when they weren't spaced out or drunk, they
were destroying stuff for kicks, drove my dogs crazy. Now
don't get me wrong, I don't hate people, I'm just not a
mixing it up kind of guy, like my own company, don't
bother anyone and they don't bother me. But when people
start messing with me, messing with my things, messing
with my life, something's got to be done...

It started with them throwing stones at the yard, busting up car windows... I let it go... Figured, they'll get bored, they'll move on... I was wrong, it escalated... Started throwing stones at my dogs, wounded them, evil little fuckers, that's when it became personal... See, like I say, I don't mix with people too well, my dogs are like my kids and these viscous little bastards were hurting them... Called the police, they weren't interested... Kids throwing stones at a scrap-yard, why would they be?

I bought a gun, planned on using it too... Caught one of the fuckers breaking into the yard, his mistake really... I know this yard... every car, every gap, every hiding place... I let him get nice and cozy in a maze of derelict cars, then took him out with crowbar to the back of the skull... Killed him outright... Didn't mean too, but shit happens right? I was sick to my stomach... I dropped the crowbar and threw up on the ground beside me... I've never so much as trapped a rat... I can't go down for this, it was an accident...
I had to think...

It's amazing how fast your mind works in an emergency... I quickly dragged him into the house and through to the bathroom, dumping him in the tub...
I stripped off his clothes and began running the water, while I nipped out to the tool shed for a hacksaw... I returned to find the bath half full. So I turned off the taps and with trembling hands, picked up the hacksaw. I squeezed my eyes tightly shut, desperately trying to wish it all away... Everything had suddenly gotten so real, there was no turning back, I'd come this far so all I could do was go on... I took a deep breath, gripped the hacksaw tightly and clenched my teeth together...

I grabbed his arm with my left hand to hold it steady and began sawing into his shoulder with the saw in my right hand. My stomach turned over at the first sight of blood as the jagged teeth tore into the flesh, almost like I was doing it to myself. The grind of the saw on bone was sickening and I hurled into the bath beside him... But I had to go on, there was no turning back now, gut wrenching as it was...

Blood poured from the open wound, diluting into the water around him... Next, I gripped his hair and sawed off his head from the back of his neck, which strangely made him seem less human without a face to look at. But I was as sick as a dog, as his apophyges had made sick, slurping, gurgling noises as it tore in two. After that, it got easier with each limb I sawed off. I pulled the plug out of the bath and began to run the shower, sadly the blood to water ratio had shifted in mass and needed cleaning before it stained. After all, I still had to shower here...

When I was left with the torso and assorted limbs, I took my meat knife and slit from the groin to the ribcage and hollowed out the corpse of organs, washing away the blood with the showerhead. I then began stripping the flesh from the bones with my knife; I just imagined I was stripping meat joints, made it a lot easier to bear.

I then, sawed up all the bones, cracking the ribs from the spine and sternum, stacking them to one side of the bath, while I loaded the joints and organs into 2 large plastic boxes. I took them downstairs to the kitchen, stacking them next to the meat grinder as I prepped it for the task ahead.

Oh, God... How had it come to this?

I set up a third plastic box to gather the mince as it fell, and proceeded to grind the flesh to mulch. I gave the dogs a bone each and left them gnaw to their hearts content, while I loaded the mince boxes onto my wheelbarrow and took them to my garden area. Then by the shovel full, I dug him into the earth, using the fork to thoroughly mix mince and mud to one. 'If nothing else, he'll make good fertilizer' I joked to myself in an effort to keep it together and get on with job at hand. I sprayed the boxes out with my garden hose over the earth before loading them back onto the wheelbarrow. I'd frozen the bones in the chest freezer, pulling a few out each day for the Jerry and Trixie. The skull, I'd boiled and sprayed with resin to make it look false and sold it on eBay as a fragile collectable for fifty three bucks by the time the bidding stopped. After all, money is money and they owe me for damages and vet bills.

A few weeks passed, the police came by asking a lot of questions, looking into a missing person's case. It was dropped soon enough though… Junky kid, always in trouble, they go missing all the time, glad to see the back of them mostly and this was no exception… I'd gotten away with it… You see, I was always brought up to be polite and have respect for authority figures; particularly officers of the law, so playing up to them had been easy. It had even given me a thrill that Jerry and Trixie were crunching down on the last of the said missing person as I saw the policemen out.

It niggled me though; that they take the time to investigate that little prick going missing but were powerless to do anything about the ongoing harassment I was still getting from his consorts.

Bloody typical…

But it turned out that their downfall would be of their own making…
They'd gotten into the habit of not only throwing stones at my property but also at passing vehicles too. No one ever stopped, people were just afraid to challenge them for fear of car jacking or worse and so it continued. Until one night, a truck was passing through… I watched the whole thing from my upstairs window.

The fucking idiots had stood in the middle of the road, all throwing stones at the front of the truck, bouncing off the windscreen and grille. The driver sounded his horn a number of times before swerving under the onslaught, catching one of them with his left bumper, knocking him over and dragging him under the front wheel. I could hear his screams above the roar of the engine, silenced only by the crack of his skull under the tyre. His whole body, a broken, mangled, bloody mess as he was crushed flat into the road by the sheer weight of the truck.

It then veered into a telegraph pole and three things happened at once. The driver launched into the windscreen, breaking his face as the glass shattered on impact, one of the two remaining pricks ran toward the truck and the telegraph pole broke in half and crashed down on the back of the tanker the truck had been ferrying. The resulting chaos that ensued happened so quickly, the tanker sprung a leak, spraying liquid nitrogen all over the prick running toward the truck. He froze instantaneously and shattered to pieces as he hit the ground due to the force of the spray.

The last of them, I saw making a break for it, the cheeky fucker was climbing over my fence into the yard. Trixie came charging out of the house, barking and growling. He picked up a wrench and hit her hard with it, there was a sickening crack as she yelped and fell to the ground unmoving. My heart missed a beat… My Trixie… My baby…

I vowed he would not see tomorrow as I bit back the tears.

I ran down the stairs, taking them two at a time, grabbed my gun, loaded it, cocked it and went to confront him. I found him out by the tool shed; he saw me and held the wrench up threateningly. 'I don't want any trouble, man. I just want to get out of here'

I smiled and shot his right knee cap, he dropped like a sack of spuds to the ground. I then strode up to him and kicked him hard in the stomach, he winced through strained breath.

'You don't want trouble? Well I'm afraid you've found it, friend'

I quickly went to the tool shed, grabbed some rope and trust him up like a prize cow.

Next, I went to Trixie and scooped her lifeless corpse up in my arms and cried into her soft fur as I brought her to him; make him see what he'd done… I gently laid her down before him… 'You want to fuck with me? You want to fuck with my life? Now you fuck with my Trixie… I'm all out of mercy friend, now you pay'

He stayed silent but fearful of my threat.

I then left the yard, ran over to the truck and climbed into the cabin to check on the driver… Dead!!!

I shook my head 'Poor bastard, another victim at the hands of these pricks.'
I quickly rummaged about in the back and found some thermos containers for storing small amounts of liquid nitrogen with other various safety equipment and garments. An idea began to form in my mind, that last prick would suffer for killing Trixie. Oh he'd pay!!!

I took the containers around to the back of the truck; it wasn't spraying so much as pouring out now. So I put on the safety gloves, mask and overcoat and quickly filled two bucket sized containers, attached the lids and headed back to Trixie's killer… Fun Time!!!

It didn't look like he'd moved while I'd been away, so I put down the containers and dragged him into the work area of the tool shed and tied him up to a dining chair stored there. Surprisingly, he didn't put up too much of a fight, figured he must have gone into shock after I shot his kneecap. I tied his wrists to the chair arms, ankles to the chair legs, then another rope over the back of his neck, under his arms, crossed at the back of the chair and looped back around the front across his chest and tied it off at the back of the chair to secure him. Nearly set… I cut off his clothes with my knife and went back outside to get the containers, hosing away the spilt blood from his gunshot wound.

Show Time!!!
I put a small coffee table beside the chair on the left and put the first container on it. I then took the lid off and untied his right arm and gripped it. I think he guessed what was coming because he began to start struggling, using all his strength to stop me dipping his hand into the container.

So I gripped his balls and squeezed hard, he froze with a sharp intake of breath and his hand sank into the liquid nitrogen.

He howled like I've never heard anyone howl before, I smiled and took his hand out. Wide eyed, he stared, mouth open in shock and burning cold pain to see his statuesque hand shining back at him. So I promptly tapped it on the arm of the chair and it shattered into many pieces on the floor.

So reeling from this, his face a mask of despair, I quickly dipped his wrist to his elbow into the container... Oh how he howled... Without awaiting a response, I tapped it on the chair arm, shattering it... Then raising the container to take his elbow to shoulder... I quickly swept up the flesh crystals from the floors and flushed them down the toilet a bit at a time. I then repeated the procedure on his left arm.

Next, his feet... It was like a foot spa; I just lifted his leg up, pushed down over the container and leaned on his knee, another howl that could shatter glass... It did amuse me slightly that when I let go of his leg, it shot into the air with such force that his foot flew off and shattered on the floor across the room... I then did his calf to his knee; he shattered that when he banged it against the chair leg... By the time I'd done both legs, swept, flushed and returned, he was positively begging for his life.

Problem was, I needed him in smaller parts or he'd melt quicker than I could flush and that could be messy and leave stains. He was sweeping up easy on the dust pan and flushing without a mess at the rate I was going. So I continued, I cut him from the chair, laid him down and poured it on him a piece at a time.

Thighs… Genitals… Ouchy!!! Kind of felt that one myself, actually winced for him… And ironically, that was the one that killed him…

He just stared wide eyed and open mouthed and I actually saw the life dim from his eyes as his soul left the coil… Like that was the moment he decided there was nothing left to live for and his soul said 'Right, I'm out of here'
My enthusiasm went as soon as his light snuffed out, it became almost mundane after that… Pour, shatter, sweep, flush and repeat…

When I'd finished flushing and tidied up, I called the police to report the accident. They called out the necessary emergency hazard services to clear away the mess, bodies, etc.
I told them I'd just heard it all out of my top window, figured it was kids fucking about and went back to sleep, previous complaints about damages supported why I'd ignore it and go back to sleep. The police apologized for the inconvenience, the truck company apologized for the stress with a few grand in compensation and the gang isn't causing me any more trouble. With the exception of Trixie, things are looking up…

Do I feel guilty about it?

Of course I do…Every day of my life, I'm still human…

Would I do it again?

Without a doubt…

Granted, I don't play well with the other children but live and let live I say...

You see, I treat people like they treat me, show respect, get respect...

Fuck with me and I'll fuck with you... I'd certainly kill for me and mine...

Thanks for listening, have a nice day, now...

Dark Confessions

...Empowerment & Redemption...

Hey friend, so you're still talking to me, huh?

I was afraid I may have frightened you off after our last chat but it's good to see you…

I suppose you'd like to hear more of Uncle Reggie's secrets would you? Well they say confession is good for the soul, you know, I like you… You're such a good listener… Feels good to get these things off my chest… As you know I don't get many visitors and although I like my own company, it does get lonely sometimes… Jerry hasn't been the same since Trixie was killed by that prick I told you about last time but he's a good dog, loyal and friendly but he's just so damn sad, it breaks my heart… But we have a new addition to the family, the scrap trade is still turning a profit and my garden area has never bloomed brighter…

You know, people bandy words like monster and cold blooded killer about but they really don't understand what makes a man tick… Let alone what drives him to protect himself or the ones he loves… I do what I do for a reason; I don't kill for the sake of it… I don't kill because I enjoy it, although I'd be lying if I said I didn't get a certain thrill from the empowerment it affords me… Like I told you before, my first kill left me sick to my stomach but it gets easier over time…Almost like an addiction… It's not so much the act as the symbolism it represents... When you think how easy it is to snuff out a candle, thus outing the flame that made it special... In essence, wiping out the endless possibilities that that soul might achieve... Such power! Such glorious power that resides in these, my hands... It feels almost Godly to wield such impact on the world yet walk in it unknown as choices of fate and justice are made…

Believe it or not I do truly believe life is precious, I just think the world is better off without some people in it... I mean don't get me wrong, I don't think I'm Judge Judy and executioner and I'm pretty tolerant until people make a conscious decision to fuck with me, then they make it personal and I got to nip it in the bud before it gets out of hand, know what I mean?

Just such an occurrence happened about eight months ago, had a couple try to scam me... Was minding my own business, sweeping up the yard, when this girl, Tess comes running through the gate, crying her eyes out, begging for my help, wanting to use my phone... She must have been mid-twenties, long dark hair, short skirt and blotchy legs with an abundance of badly applied make up that attempted to hide bruises... I'm always ready to help someone in need so I let her in, gave her the phone and went to the kitchen to make some coffee...

When I came back in, I caught her pouring what looked like blood from a small bottle all around her nose and mouth, confused the hell out of me... Next thing I know, she's running out the door into the yard, screaming and shouting to be left alone, of course I went after her in concern, after all, I didn't have a clue what was happening... Figured she was care in the community or something... It was then that I saw her accomplice at the gate, filming her running out, covered in blood and me following... Now that's got to look bad... He must have been early thirties, greased hair, thin pencil moustache and large buck teeth, dressed in a shirt, jacket and slacks... He had one of those smug, toothy smiles that swings on my tit and makes my blood boil...

Next thing I know is he's threatening to go to the police with his video evidence and she's ready to testify that I'd tried to rape her unless I can come up with some money… Like I say about conscious decisions, you got to nip them in the bud right? To my mind, they'd already signed their own death warrants and forfeited any mercy in one act of deception with the hope of extortion… I'm not a ruthless man but I won't be fucked with… Treat me with respect and you'll be afforded the same courtesy, fuck with me and your arse is mine and not in a nice way… So they left, thinking they had the upper hand and told me I'd be hearing from them when they'd decided how much they wanted from me… All part of the plan, standard blackmail scam, make me worry, leave me think on it, make me think I'm in trouble so I'll get the money together… Make a payment, then they'll want more… I won't play these games and they clearly had no idea who they were fucking with…

Unknown to them, I followed them into town… There's only one road from my scrap yard and I know a short cut to where it leads, so on bicycle I was in town before them and watched them pull up into a cheap motel from a petrol station across the street and waited for them to enter their room before I nipped across the road to their car and slipped on my gloves… Conveniently for me, they had left it unlocked so I quickly opened door and rummaged through the glove box and found some documents and a number of different false identities with their pictures on… Just like I figured, professional scammers, always out to make a buck at some other poor bugger's expense…

I then headed to their room and loitered around outside, affording myself brief glimpses through their window, know your enemy 101... I could hear a lot of shouting and banging about so I moved closer to the window for a better look; he was knocking the shit out of her... I got to disliking him more and more... The general gist of their arguing was that she should do as she's told and there was no way out for her... It finally ended with her as a sobbing mess on the floor as he sat in the chair, popped a beer and switched on the TV... I figured she's paying the price for this life style but strangely it put doubts in mind about killing her... Actually caused quite the moral quandary for me, I sympathized with her but if I'd let her live, she could blackmail me... I just wasn't seeing any middle ground on this one...

So now I had a location to find them, I had to plan my strategy for killing them and disposing of them without raising any suspicions... After all, never let it be said that I don't cover my tracks thoroughly... I'm not like those serial killers that do it for notoriety or fame or ego. Those guys are idiots, they get sloppy, think they're clever leaving messages and clues for the police to find... No thank you, I like my freedom too much and unlike them I'm doing a public service, disposing of humanity's pond scum... I figured take him down and she'll do as she's told, basic psychology, make her oppressor look weak and she'll follow the dominant aggressor... At least that's the theory... So I nipped back home on my bicycle, got my gun, scalpel and masking tape and headed back to them...

Again I waited around outside their room and built up my adrenaline before knocking. 'Who is it?' I heard him call from behind the door. 'Room service' I replied and as soon as the door was open a crack; I kicked it as hard as I could, sending him sprawling to the floor as his face rebounded off the wood. I then charged into the room, gun in hand and closed the door behind me, quickly covering the pair of them. She let out a cry as I grabbed her roughly by the arm and threw her to the floor to join him before shutting the curtains. He grinned that smug smile that annoys me so much as he wiped the blood from his lip. 'What do you think you're going to accomplish by this? It changes nothing' he gloated. So I stepped forward and pistol whipped the fucker, soon wiped the smile from his face which brought a huge grin to mine. He glared at me through evil eyes as I laughed in his face, bringing the gun up to cover him again as the girl began to sob.

I figured it was time to bring some psychology into the mix and grabbed her by the hair. 'Get on your knees' I growled at her, she quickly did as she was told before me and began to tremble and panic as I put the gun to her head and cocked it. 'Give me the camera or I'll kill her' I said to him as tears streamed down her face 'Please... give him the camera' she choked. 'Fuck you, kill her, I don't give a fuck... The video is already on my lap top and I'll still be wanting my money' he smiled smugly. Her face dropped in fear and shock at his response and her believed imminent death. I took the gun away from her head and pushed her over with my foot 'And you stay with this guy?' I queried of her. Divide and conquer as they say. She digested the information, still shaking as she shot him a dirty look. 'Hey chill Babe, I knew he wouldn't kill you, he hasn't got the balls' he smiled smarmily again.

She looked back to me in confusion 'You really believe that? He'd have seen you dead without a second thought'.

I then took the masking tape from my pocket and threw it to her 'Tape him up; we're going for a ride'. She looked to him worried; he just smiled and shook his head. 'We're not going anywhere, what's he going to do? Kill us? I don't think so' he said getting to his feet. I calmly took the scalpel from my pocket, stepped forward and sharply jabbed it into his shoulder. The shock on his face was priceless as he dropped to his knees and she cried out. 'I'm not fucking about, now tape him up' I growled as I aimed the gun at her. She quickly taped his hands behind his back and his ankles together with him giving very little resistance. Luckily most of his blood soaked into his shirt, the rest into the motel flannel I applied to the wound. After all, I couldn't be leaving any evidence of foul play behind when we left… Finally I got her to tape his mouth too and then sit beside him while I looked outside to check the coast was clear… When I was happy there were no people or passing traffic, I made him stand and threw him over my shoulder and had her lead the way at gunpoint with the camera and laptop to their car… She then opened the trunk and I quickly dumped him into it and slammed it shut and made her get into the driving seat as I sat in the back… She gunned the engine and we were soon heading away back to my place as I kept the gun trained on her from the seat behind…

As we got back to the yard, I made her park up next to my tool shed, got out and ushered her through the door to the work area. I fully expected her to try to make a run for it when I went out to get him from the trunk but she didn't, she'd waited as she'd been told.

Her eyes were red and tear stained and her features were gaunt, looking for all the world like little girl lost waiting to be told what to do… He put up a bit of a struggle as I tried to pull him from the car, the fucker actually kicked me full pelt as I opened the trunk. Took me by surprise too, I don't know what he thought he was going to achieve, he was still bound as tightly as when we'd left. I just grabbed his feet and dragged him out, his body hitting the ground with such a thud as to wind him with the impact and dragged him indoors breathless and wheezing…

Next I laid down some plastic sheeting and sat a chair in its middle before lifting him bodily to his feet and plonking him onto it… He put up very little resistance to me tying him to the chair, still dazed and winded as he was… She'd barely moved, just walked around in circles, oblivious to what was going on as I secured his ropes… He then started to come around as I ripped the tape from his mouth, tearing half his tash with it… It was then that he began to test the ropes that bound him. And then again with that smile as he tried to reassert his cockiness 'So what's this? More scare tactics? I got to say, I'm not impressed' he grinned smugly. I had to get rid of that smile; it was just winding me up. So I took off my belt, looped it around one of the bars at the back of the chair, grabbed his hair, yanked back his head and looped the belt across his forehead and tightened it so he couldn't move.

He cursed and shouted but he wasn't going anywhere. I then grabbed a hammer and chisel from the workbench, lined the chisel's blade up to the line where his top teeth met his gums and banged down hard on it with the hammer as his teeth shattered with the impact.

He gargled a scream through the blood and tooth fragments that quickly filled his mouth so I un-strapped the belt from his forehead and allowed him to spit out the contents of his mouth… After all I didn't want him choking on blood and teeth, we were just getting started. Also I needed my belt, it could be embarrassing if my trousers fell down. Would kind of kill my credibility…

For the first time, I saw true fear in his eyes and that grin would task me no more… He began to freak out, rocking the chair back and forth, so I figured I'd better restrict his movement some more… I went back to the workbench and picked up my electric drill, plugged it in, went behind him and dropped to one knee as I lined the drill up with his lower spine… Then happy I'd found the right spot, I hit the drill's power button and pressed it into his spine as it roared to life and sank into the flesh as he howled to the sound of the drill grinding into bone 'til his legs just twitched as his spinal cord was severed.

The girl was still walking around in circles, humming a soft tune to herself as she had clearly gone to her happy place. I figured it was time for her to join in the fun; justice is a bitch ain't it? But trust me; it's not what you think… I wanted her to find her own justice and free herself from his thrall; I wanted to empower her… And the only way I could think of to find a middle ground was for her to lose her fear of him and become like me to he who had wronged her… 'What's your name?' I asked of her. It took a few moments for her to register that I'd spoken to her.
'Tess…' she whimpered softly with a far away look in her eyes.
'Well Tess, don't worry' I said gently 'I'm not going to hurt you… I want to free you'

So I led her to the workbench, showed her all the tools and implements at her disposal then pointed to him 'Or rather, I want you to free yourself, so that he can't hurt you anymore' I continued.

He just sobbed. I mean don't get me wrong, I'm not an idiot, I kept the gun trained on her the whole time in case she turned on me. I then stepped back to the door to see what she would do…

For a long while she didn't do anything, just stood before him as he tried to intimidate her and manipulate her with begs, pleas and shouts of how much trouble she'd be in… Then just when I thought I'd better step in, she walked to the workbench, picked up a staple gun and walked back to him. She then pursed his lips between her finger and thumb and proceeded to staple them together. As she let go, blood spat through the gaps as he sobbed. Tears of pain and fear welled in his red-rimmed eyes as he realized he could no longer control her and he was now at her mercy. And for the first time, she smiled and walked back to the workbench, this time she picked up pliers. She walked back to him, kneeled before him and proceeded to unbutton his shirt, revealing the nipple rings that glinted in the light. In turn, she gripped each one gently with the pliers before ripping them out savagely. He let out a scream that tore his lips to shreds around the staples and so his arms struggled against the ropes…

She then took the drill from the work bench, still plugged in from when I had used it, she lifted his elbow slightly and he roared as she hit the power button as it bore into his armpit, grinding through the bone until the tip spun through the shirt on his shoulder.

'I'll have to balance you out' she said with a sad smile and did the same to his other armpit. Again he roared and cried, so she picked up a monkey wrench and swinging it, she shattered his jaw with it. It hung at a peculiar angle and she scrutinized him like an artist whose piece is missing something that quickly came to her. She took a large hacksaw from the workbench, gripped his hair, pulled back his head and began sawing across his mouth, tearing his cheeks in half to his hoarse cries.

As she let go of his hair, his head came up and his jaw hung vertically with his chin bouncing off his Adam's apple, his bottom teeth looking like a bizarre horse shoe embedded in flesh upon his neck while his throat made rasping noises, unable to breathe properly as his tongue was dragged down by the weight of his jaw… It didn't half put a shiver up my spine, even made me feel a bit queasy if I'm honest… Damn, she's good…

There was no stopping her now, she moved almost fluidly as she used a Stanley blade to cut out his tongue, then brought his jaw up to its natural position and used a nail gun to clamp flesh and bone back together across his mouth line. Finally, she cut him from the chair, laid him on his back and sat astride him, looking eagerly into his eyes, smiling as he gurgled and coughed, drowning in his own blood… 'You have no power over me, finally… I'm free'. She took a pencil from her pocket, turned his head to the side, put it in his ear and banged it just enough to shatter his eardrum. He shook violently, so she banged it all the way in, hoping that it would be the killing blow… But he still shook, so she calmly stood and went back to the workbench, picked up a Stanley blade and slit his throat with it to be sure… And so his body rasped its last breath… 'Goodbye' she whispered and gently kissed his forehead…

She then stood and looked to me with a gentle smile… My blood ran cold as she walked toward me, I couldn't even bring myself to raise the gun… The bitch scared the hell out of me… But she simply hugged me 'Thank you' she soothed then dropped to her knees and moved my gun hand to her head 'You can kill me now' I looked to her puzzled. 'I don't want to kill you Tess, you're free to go'.

She stood and kissed my cheek 'I don't have anywhere to go, can I stay with you?'
I agreed to a trial period which seemed to make her happy and it certainly made short work disposing of the body with an extra pair of hands… Well I told you last time how I do that, why mess with what works? Like I say, my garden area has never bloomed brighter... Here we are eight months on and we couldn't be happier, there will always be people who want to fuck with us and dealing with them is something we enjoy doing together as a couple…

Awww... You got to go huh?

Well no problem, there's always next time, it was good to see you…

And thanks for listening…

Have a nice day now…

Dark Confessions
…Of Justice & betrayal…

You're back again???

My, my, you're eager… So what can I do you for, Friend?
More stories huh? Tell me, what makes you keep coming
back for more? Morbid curiosity or a need to learn? You
look puzzled, could it be you don't know? Well don't let it
stress you, let me tell you about this brother and sister act
that blew through here a while back and upset the little
lady… You haven't met her yet have you? Her name's
Tess, she's a feisty little thing, remember I told you about
her last time? Trust me when I tell you, you don't want to
get on the wrong side of her… You know that old saying
"Hell hath no fury like a woman scorned?" Well I have
never known such an apt saying apply to anyone so
accurately… The bitch is crazy but I wouldn't have the
balls to tell her that to her face… You've got to admire that
kind of fear…

Never did I think when I first laid eyes on her that I would
come to love her as I have… Its like a mutual respect, I
gave her the means to free herself and she was thankful,
didn't want to leave… I was reluctant at first, but in turn,
she's given me companionship, never had it before and you
can't miss what you've never had… And Jerry loves her to
bits too, she spoils the old dog and he can't get enough of
that… She's given my life new meaning, new purpose and
she makes me laugh… And between you and me, she's a
dynamo in the sack…

  Anyway, pardon my smile, I digress… Where was I? Arr
yes… A brother and sister moved in around here, well I say
moved in, they parked a caravan in the lot opposite the
yard… Seemed nice enough, very friendly, waved and
smiled a lot…

And I remember, there was this one day, Tess had insisted I take her to a bar; the damn woman got it in her head she was going to teach me about socializing... I don't do bars; rarely drink, when you lead a life like I do, its better to keep a clear head... But like most things with her, she nagged my fucking head off 'til I found myself sat at a table in a bar, cradling a glass wondering how the fuck I had got there... I mean, when did no stop meaning no?

Anyway, when I'd relaxed enough to start looking around me, I began to notice all the traits that make me do what I do... Drug pushers... Greed... Selfishness... Aggression... I shook my head; this was a den of iniquity... Even saw a guy at the bar slip something into a woman's drink when she went to the bathroom... I told Tess and her eyes narrowed and I smiled as I saw the fire ignite in her... Seemed I was to have some work to do after all today... So just to keep a low profile, I sent her over to flirt with him briefly as a distraction as I swapped their drinks over, they were both on orange Alco-pops, so it was no biggie...

Everything went to plan, we sat back at our table and watched and waited as the woman came back from the bathroom and finished up her drink as the guy got progressively drowsy 'til he collapsed and fell off his bar stool into a heap on the floor. The woman panicked and Tess and I leapt to her aid and helped her to get him outside. We played up to her with sympathy and concern as we asked her questions 'Is he okay? Is he on any meds?'

Of course, she confessed she'd only just met the guy and began searching his pockets for meds at our questioning. Then with a rattle, she pulled out a bottle of pills and read the label "Rohypnol".

I could tell by the look on her face that she had began to piece together the guy's intentions toward her and was quickly repulsed by him. She stood up and stepped away 'Bastard!' she exclaimed through clenched teeth 'He's a fucking rapist'. We played total innocence 'Really? That's terrible, what should we do with him? Should we call an ambulance?' Tess asked sympathetically. I could barely keep a straight face.
'Do what you like with him, I'm leaving' she replied angrily and walked away.

Great choice of words, felt like a green light… ☺
I took his car keys from his pocket, hit the lock button and waited to hear the beep and click of his car in the parking lot. We bundled him into our car and Tess took him away as I drove his car. After all, an abandoned car could raise a few questions and you've got to cover your tracks.

It didn't take us long to get him back to our place and we have a new car into the bargain too, just change the number plates and we're good to go. I moved him into my work area, quickly tied his hands behind his back and bound his feet together as he began to stir. Then hooking his feet to an engine crane, I hit the button and with a whirring, buzzing sound, he rose into the air, hanging upside down by his feet as his face went red as the blood rushed to his head. Seemed just the ticket to wake him from his groggy state, he desperately looked around him in confusion and panic as I laid down a few meters of plastic sheeting beneath him.

My mind ran over with possibilities of what I should do to him. Truth is, I ain't never had a rapist through here before so I don't really know how to distribute punishment before I kill him.

I mean, I read this book **'Fear the Reaper'** by a guy called
Fritz O'Skennick a while back and he raped a guy with
the hammer's shaft before pulling his plums out through a
slit in his scrotum for raping his girlfriend. But it just don't
feel like my style, seems a bit on the nose to me. Besides, I
know Tess has a few ideas on this one, so I'll just wait to
see what she says.

'What's going on? Where am I?' he suddenly asked, a bit
spooked. I smiled at him before answering.
'Good question Friend, but don't let it worry you; it'll all
be over soon enough'
'Did Mikey send you? The money is in the car, just take it
and let me go'
'I don't know anything about no money; do date rape drugs
and orange Alco-pops ring any bells with you?'
'What? You got to get me down, it's not safe'
'Don't worry yourself; I know the little lady will be
wanting a few words with you'
'You don't understand, they're going to be looking for me,
I've got to get out of here.'
'Then I'm afraid it ain't your day Friend, nobody knows
you're here so no one's going to come looking'

Without warning, the door creaked open and Tess entered
looking a little nervous as she beckoned me over. As I
approached, she began to whisper hurriedly.
'Reggie, you've got to finish up here quickly and quietly,
we've got company'. I looked at her agasp.
'Company? What company?'
'New neighbors, they've moved into the lot across the road,
decided to come over and meet us. They've brought a
muffin basket'
'What? You're kidding? Who does that?'

'I think it's what normal people do. Just finish up quickly and come and meet them, we don't want to raise any suspicions.'

'Okay, I'll be with you soon' I replied and kissed her before she left through the door from whence she came… I then grabbed a large plastic box, picked up my Stanley knife from the workbench and walked over to him… I put the plastic box under him, hit the button on the engine crane to lower him so his head was just above the box and knelt beside him…

'What are you doing?' he asked in confusion and a little fear…

'I had a few things I wanted to impart to you in regard to your conduct but I'm afraid I've got to cut this chit-chat short, if you'll pardon the pun' I said smiling as I slit his throat. He gargled and hissed as blood pumped over his face and flowed into the box beneath him as his body twitched like a fish on a line…

I quickly switched off the lights, shut and locked the door and went to the bathroom to wash my face and hands. I checked my clothes in the mirror as I dried myself with the towel. Yes, I looked suitably presentable, another perk of having Tess in my life, I actually care about my appearance now. It was never an issue for me before, wore the same stained clothes, day in and day out, I wasn't out to impress anyone so it didn't matter much to me. She's even got me brushing my hair and shaving regularly coz she don't like my stubble. The more I think about it, the more I can see how domesticated this damn woman has made me. I mean even my living area has such feminine overtones to it. I now have curtains instead of a blanket nailed to the wall and what is the deal with cushions?

I can't think of any purpose they serve, you sit down and you move them to make room. It don't make sense but it seems to make her happy, so I guess I can't really complain… Just pisses me off sometimes, coz it doesn't feel like my home anymore… But I guess that's the price of sharing your life with someone…

As I left the bathroom, I took a deep breath, time to meet the neighbors, guess she's going to have me socializing after all… I stepped into the room and immediately felt overwhelmed. I'm just not used to hosting guests outside of the ones that piss me off… The guy was on his feet in a second with his arm outstretched, I had to resist the impulse to knock him on his arse, coming at me like that… Kind of got my back up as my instincts kicked in… But he was friendly enough, big smile and a strong handshake as he introduced them… If anything, Jerry was more laid back than I was, some guard dog huh? Sat back there like lord muck as they scratched his ear and got his leg tapping a beat on the floor…

'Hi, you must be Reggie, I'm Charles and this is my dear sister Leticia' he said gesturing to her.
'You can call me Tish' she added, stepping over to shake my hand too…
'Hi, good to meet you, can I get you anything?' I replied uncomfortably.
'No, we're fine thank you. Your good lady made us a lovely coffee to have with our muffins' he laughed.

And so on it went, exchanging pleasantries and stories 'til I eventually relaxed enough to feel reasonably comfortable.

They seemed like good people but I think I could have done with the socializing thing in smaller steps to be honest. Finally they left and we waved them off at the door before coming in…

'Well?' Tess queried of me as we sat.
'Well what?' I answered, completely confused.
'What did you think of them?'
'I don't know, they seem nice enough' I shrugged.
'A little too nice I think'
'I don't understand'
'Something seemed off with them, like they were digging for an angle'
'What do you mean?'
'As you know, I used to be with a scam artist so I know the signs. They were too nice, too keen, they were like Mormons but we know they weren't'
'So what do you think they're doing?'
'I'm not sure… Casing the joint… Working a con… I don't know yet but I'll think on it'
'You do that' I smiled. She then sidled over to me, hugged me and kissed me on the cheek. I kissed her back before asking 'What was that for?'
'Coz I'm proud of you'
'For what?'
'You made a huge effort in socializing with them and I know how hard that must have been for you, I love you'
'I love you too' I replied as she climbed atop me and sat astride my waist before looking deeply into my eyes and kissing me passionately. I won't go into details of what followed but needless to say, a good time was had by all. A gentleman never tells and all that… Pardon my grin…

Later that night, it occurred to me that the guy I'd killed earlier had said something about money in the car. So finally my curiosity got the better of me and I nipped out to have a look. After a bit of a rummage around, I found a large case in the boot, opened it and quickly closed it again as my breath caught in my throat… I tucked it under my arm and ran into the house with it…

I quickly called Tess as I sat at the table, took a deep breath and opened it once more. There was about a million in cash, neat, crisp bills in bundles of ten thousand.
Tess was speechless, then thoughtful, then very excited at the possibilities this held for us. I couldn't help but get lost in the euphoria of her excitement and if I'm honest, a good few daydreams of my own… And although this led to some more fantastic sex, we realized that the guy might have been right, someone was bound to come looking for it…

First things first, we had to get rid of the car and the body… The crusher made short work of the car and we got rid of the body in our usual manner. We've even had to extend the garden area and dig the minced flesh deeper into the earth. The garden is absolutely beautiful and we love being out there on the sunnier days. And of course, Tess finds it very therapeutic and has developed quite the green thumb. She's even started growing some vegetables in the extended area and in fairness to her, there's nothing like home grown veg… And Tess' is the best…

We'd even thought of entering them into some local vegetable contest but were bound to get a bit sketchy when they started asking about growing tips and fertilizer… Never mind, maybe one day…

Sorry, I digress again… Everything was quiet for the next month or two, Charles and Tish came over regularly which kind of helped me learn how to deal with people on a sociable level and Tess had people other than me to talk too and she began putting her initial suspicions down to paranoia…

But as time went on, we started to notice a lot of little things going missing here and there… Jewelry, CD's, DVD's and even items of clothing but still we put it down to having misplaced them…
Probably naïve of us but we so wanted to believe our new friends were just that, friends…

In fact, it was purely by accident that we found out they were stealing from us… Tess called over to see them one day and Tish was wearing her missing bracelet, which again awoke her suspicions… So as Tish went out to make a coffee, Tess had a nose around the room and discovered a number of our missing DVD's in their collection, one even had my name on as a gift from Tess… As you can imagine, she was absolutely fuming but kept her cool for the duration of the time she was there and told me about it when she got home…

Now I know how hypocritical it sounds that we were upset that someone was stealing from us, given that we were sitting on one million in cash that was clearly ill gotten gains but there's a principal involved… They were our friends, we'd welcomed them into our home, we'd shared a lot of time and a lot of laughter with them, we'd been there for them, so in turn, we had come to expect a certain level of loyalty from them… And that is why the betrayal had cut so much deeper…

But still we wanted to give them the benefit of the doubt, maybe we lent them the movies and forgot, maybe Tess had lent her the bracelet one night when they'd been drinking... So we waited for them to go out one day, and Tess shinnied in through a loose window on the side of the caravan and let me in through the door... Much to our disappointment, it was as we'd expected, our clothes in their washing; Tess' jewelry in a jewelry box in the bedroom, my two signed **'Fractured Persona'** albums in their CD collection, there was no doubt anymore...

We went back home to try to work out how we were going to deal with this... Of course, Tess' initial thought was to set their caravan on fire and burn them alive as they slept (She frightens me sometimes)... But she realized that that would draw attention to us with them living so close... When she'd calmed down enough to think of it rationally, it caused us quite the moral quandary. We'd actually come to care for them... We didn't want to cause them harm but this matter of betrayal would have to be addressed and though we knew it had to be done, neither of our hearts were truly in it... I guess this is what happens when you let people get too close...

In the end we settled on the idea of letting them explain themselves on our terms... So we invited them over for a coffee and laced their drinks with Rohypnol. As soon as they passed out, I tied them into chairs in my work area as Tess nipped over to their place and reclaimed our possessions to present to them as evidence when we began questioning them... I don't mind admitting I felt nervous, I didn't want to do this but they'd forced our hand and we couldn't let it continue...

There was a principal involved, a principal of justice and betrayal, a principal of friendship and boundaries and if nothing else, then to make the point that we won't be fucked around with by people who claim to be our friends... There was a penance to pay...

After I'd laid down the plastic sheeting, we placed them at opposite ends of the room facing one another, taped each of their mouths and put a table in the middle of the room with our stolen possessions on...
We figured I'd deal with Charles and Tess would deal with Tish... We then turned out the lights and left the room, kind of give them an air of uncertainty to wake to...

Finally they woke as we heard some attempts at shifting about from beyond the door... So we stepped into the room without saying a word and switched on the light...
They squinted as their eyes adjusted to the light and widened pleadingly as they saw us... I pushed the light bulb that hung on a long cord from the ceiling so it would give an unnerving effect as it threw each of them into shadow and light as it swung back and forth... Tess walked over and stood beside Tish as I approached Charles... I ripped the tape from his mouth and he actually looked relieved to see me...

'Reggie, thank God you're here, can you untie me and we'll get out of here'
The poor bastard actually thought I was here to rescue him.
'Where do you think you are Charles?'
'I don't know, I can't remember anything... We were having coffee... Then we were... here...'

I walked over to the table and began picking up some of the items for him to see without a word… The change in his facial expression told me realization had dawned…

'Okay Charles, would you care to explain why you and Tish have been stealing from us?'

'What? Uh… We haven't… We borrowed a few things, maybe we should have asked…'

'Maybe you should have Charles, you see Tess and I have grown very fond of you and your sister and it breaks our hearts that it has come to this'

'Wait a minute… You must have broken into our place to get these things back… How dare you pull this shit when you are no better???' He tried in an effort to take a moral high ground… I moved in close 'til our noses were almost touching. 'Don't you dare try to turn this around on us… We welcomed you into our home, we offered you friendship and you repay us in betrayal' I growled and then looked to Tess 'If would my Love…'

Tess walked to the workbench, picked up a hacksaw and strolled casually back to Tish… Then using her left hand to hold Tish's hand straight on the chair arm, she began sawing into her wrist… Tish shifted uncomfortably in the chair as her knees jigged, toes curled and tears streamed down her face as she made the most bizarre muffled elephant noises as she tried to scream through the tape as the teeth of the saw tore through flesh and bone with a sickening, grinding noise…

Helplessly Charles screamed 'NOOOOO' I looked at him and smiled 'See, that's the difference between me and Tess, personally I'd have used an axe or meat cleaver… Much quicker and a cleaner cut but I guess it's those little differences that keep a guy interested, huh?' I laughed.

I walked over to Tess and kissed her as Tish's hand hit the floor with a squelchy thud… Tess went back to the workbench and exchanged the hacksaw for a blow torch and sparked it to flame…

'What's she doing?' cried Charles in alarm as I grabbed a meat cleaver from the workbench and strode back to him… 'She's got to cauterize the wound less your dear sister will die of blood loss' I smiled…
Tess then brought the white flame to Tish's bloody stump and let it dance and sizzle over the flesh… It was at this point that Tish passed out in shock as her body shook… By this time, Charles was positively crying his eyes out with sobs of 'NOOOOOO' 'You're crazy' 'Please stop this' and 'Don't hurt her anymore'

I kind of saw this as my cue, my time to shine, so to speak…
'She's safe for now Charles, she's clearly gone to her happy place… Gives us guys a chance to chat' I grinned…
'This is madness… How can you do this???'
'Oh Charles, Charles, Charles… I was about to ask that very same question of you… In answer to your question, the loss of a hand as punishment for theft has been used for centuries and is in fact still practiced in some Middle Eastern countries… It makes for a wonderful deterrent'
'It's barbaric'
'Trust me when I tell you that this is incredibly civilized compared to the punishment of others who have pissed us off or tried to fuck us over… We liked you both, we considered you our friends so believe me, we are being incredibly lenient with you… So now I ask you, how could you steal from us? We trusted you… we loved you…'

'It was never personal… For what it's worth, we liked you too'

'How can it not be personal? You stole from us after we accepted you as our friends, you betrayed us'

'What do you want me to say? It's in our nature? It's how we were brought up? I don't know… What do you want from me???'

'I want the truth…'

'The truth? We are impulsive, we see something we like, we take it, we get a thrill from the act… Something I'm very sure you can relate too, judging by the familiarity this scenario shines you in…'

'And again, you try to turn it around on me… The difference between us Charles, is that my impulses only rise when others draw them out… You have brought this on yourself' I replied, raising the meat cleaver and bringing it down on his wrist which pumped his blood as his hand hit the floor with a fleshy thump… He huffed and puffed as he sucked and blew air through his teeth as his face scrunched up…

Tess walked over and exchanged the meat cleaver for the blow torch with me… Charles then looked up to me…

'Can you truly say things would have been different if we hadn't stolen from you? What if our music had been too loud? What if our coffee wasn't to your liking? What then?'

'What is your point Charles?'

'My point is that you judge us on our nature without reflection of your own… It would have always ended like this regardless of circumstance…'

'Well I guess we'll never know for sure now, will we?'

I knelt beside him and cauterized his stump with the blow-torch as he danced uncomfortably in the chair before passing out… But his words seemed to bounce around in my mind as the barbeque smell of roasting flesh invaded my nostrils with its heady scent… Could he be right? Do I just validate my impulses in a delusion to absolve my actions? Or is there justification in the acts that bind me to this path? Something to think on I guess…

I must confess, this whole affair had caused quite a predicament for us… I don't know whether it was sentimentality or maybe his words had struck a nerve but we couldn't bring ourselves to kill them yet we couldn't think of what to do with them either… Obviously, we couldn't let them go, so for the time being, we locked them up, her in the attic room and him in the basement to think things over… We kept them apart to let them wonder and worry about each other… Basic psychology, their first concern would be for each other which makes for a distraction from the fear and anger they would have been feeling…

We fed them, gave them the means to wash, gave them clean clothes and finally when relations became a strained civility, we reunited them… They were incredibly grateful and though they accepted their fate as our prisoners, they knew we didn't wish them any further harm… Justice had been served and punishment swiftly distributed and we had let them live…

This was all very new to me, I hadn't had friends before and I'd started to feel a strange mix of emotions that were alien to me… It was unpleasant, it gave me a knot in my stomach… I think it was… remorse…

…I was actually feeling regret of my actions…

…Most bizarre…

Now I know what you're thinking, Reggie is going soft and in some ways you'd probably be right… But let me tell you something, Karma is a strange mistress, what goes around certainly comes around… You live by the sword, you'll die by the sword and we were certainly testament to that… And though Tess and I stood at a juncture of potential growth and change in the way we conduct ourselves in the face of those who trespass against us, unknown to us, events were already in motion that would have us fighting for our lives…

I mean, we really did want to change, we genuinely wanted to be better people but the past has a way of catching up with you as it collides with the future and forces you down a dark path that very few could ever return from… Our biggest challenge was yet to come…

Oh yes, what happened about the money? I was wondering when you'd ask me about that…

Well Friend, I'll tell you about that next time, I'm afraid time is ticking on and I have places to be…
So I shall have to bid you farewell…

Have a great day now…

And thanks for listening…

Dark Confessions
...Of Men & Money...

Wow, you're back so soon… You couldn't wait, huh?

Well it's good to see you…
I suppose you'll be wanting to hear more about the events
that followed our last escapade and of course, the money
and all the shit that caused us… I just hope I didn't build it
up too much for you, there's nothing worse than the
disappointment of high expectations unattained…

Now where was I? Ah yes, we were wondering what to do
about Charles and Tish and dealing with a few regrets of
how we'd handled the situation… As you can imagine,
things were a bit fraught in the beginning… There was an
unspoken tension, an atmosphere you could cut with a knife
without anyone having to utter a word… Even after we'd
given them the run of the house and released them from the
basement, they held what can only be described as a
passive defiance to their captivity… It does make me smile
on reflection how Charles could make the intonation of
'Hello' sound so much like 'Fuck you'…

It took time but we did eventually find a middle ground to
start building trust again… Basically, after a few months,
we had it out and everyone voiced their grievances over
what had happened… Tess and I apologized for cutting
their hands off and they in turn apologized for stealing from
us and were grateful that we hadn't killed them… We kind
of explained to them that if they had been anyone else, we
wouldn't be having the conversation and they would be
doing a tour of duty as fertilizer in the garden area… They
went quiet for a while after that but I think they understood
the relevance of our restraint…

What we didn't know while we were sorting out our domestic problems, was that the owners of the money we'd got from that date rapist I'd killed when we first met Charles and Tish were on the war path and keen to get the said money back... In hindsight, if I'd lost a million in cash, I'd probably be keen to track it down too... Apparently, they'd checked the security cameras in the parking lot at the bar where we'd taken the guy... They were in fact the bar's owners and much to our dismay, they were mobsters... Kind of had their fingers in every pie of organized crime in the local area, Racketeering, prostitution, human trafficking... you name it, they had a stake in it... Like I said before 'It was a den of iniquity'...

They'd tracked down the girl we'd helped and they'd mercilessly beaten her to death just to confirm she'd never seen us before... They'd used our blurry pictures from the security footage and had been searching for months for anybody who knew who we were... Took them a long while coz nobody really knows us, they just got lucky one day when they came across a cashier at our local supermarket who recognized us as the couple who own the scrap yard... Sadly, what she thought was her good deed of the day ended up costing her, her life when they shot her in the face to cover their own tracks... I guess their logic was if she could recognize us and tell them, she could do the same to them... Vicious circle...

And to be honest, they couldn't have come at a worse time, everything was starting to calm down with Charles and Tish... We had even started letting them into the yard with accompanied visits to their caravan to get things they were going to need from day to day...

And of course to make it more homely for them to have their possessions around them when we gave them a bedroom each… In a strange way, they seemed quite thankful to have a roof over their heads as opposed to being stuck in a leaky caravan… Yes, things were certainly getting better… We'd even bought them prosthetic hands with a small dip into the million… And they were learning to control them slowly but like a lot of things, it takes time and patience…

We were keen to start our new life, turn over a new leaf and put the past behind us, but as is with these things, fate is always there to deal its blow and I don't mean it has a big bag of hash to sell you… We were on the path to change, it just seemed that life had other plans for us and we'd be forced to embrace our true nature regardless of how deep we buried it or how many masks we wore to hide it…

I remember the morning well, we'd all sat down to a hearty breakfast and Jerry was begging for scraps at the table. It was nice, it was normal and it promised to be a pleasant day… The sun was out for a change and Tess was going to take Tish into town to do some shopping while Charles helped me at the yard… We'd figured, if they were going to live with us, we had to loosen the leash a little and include them more in the running of the house and the yard… Kind of like a trust exercise, make them feel more at home so to speak…

Anyway, the girls went off shopping, leaving me and Charles to sort out a few customers that came and went as the morning wore on… Car parts mainly, so it was easy money, most of the cars are already stripped down so I just give them what they need, they pay and they're gone…

Charles was pretty attentive, watching how I dealt with the customers, looking over the car parts and learning his way around the yard, kind of felt like my apprentice…
Never been a mentor before, the very idea made me giggle muchly…

Around about 10:30am, I happened to notice a car drive into one of the old building premises on the industrial estate… Like I told you before the estate is abandoned, has been for a long while, so not many people pass through here unless they're coming to us… My initial reaction was one of suspicion, figured it was the old Reggie resurfacing, so I put it to the back of my mind and thought no more of it… The new Reggie was a better man than that… But sadly the new Reggie was also sat in a bubble of delusional transition and couldn't see the warning signs of a potential threat when it was right in front of his eyes…

Just after 11am, two cars came into view on the dirt road, even at a distance I could tell they weren't likely to be customers… The cars looked like they'd just rolled off the showroom floor and anyone with that kind of money is not going to needing anything in trade from the likes of me… The alarm bells were wailing in my head like klaxons… At this point, new Reggie found he was out of his depth and sensibly took a back seat as I reasserted myself to my default setting… My first thoughts were 'They are either government, police or gangsters'. Although I think I could rule out government, I'm just not important enough to be a threat… My next thought was 'Get my gun'… The next test will be when they get out of their cars at the gate…

When they pulled up and got out, I discovered there were eight of them and all were wearing suits, so that didn't really help either… It's a sign of the times when you can't tell the good guys from the bad guys 'til its too late… Just got to play it by ear and see what they want, although part of me already knew it was about the money… But again, whose interest? Police or gangsters? I told Charles to go into the house with Jerry and not make a noise and quickly gave him my gun 'If anyone comes in after you, cock it, aim and pull the trigger' he looked at me stunned
'I've never fired a gun in my life'
'You may not have to yet, it's just a precaution, your life may depend on it'
He nodded, grabbed Jerry by the collar and quickly led him into the house…

As they approached the gate, I walked up to greet them…
'What can I do you for Friend?' I asked jovially of the one who appeared to be in charge… He looked a bit of a cocky fucker, strolling around like he owned the place, again, could be police or gangster…

'You own this place?' he replied.
'Yep, all my life and my father before me' I smiled. He took a phone from his pocket, hit a button and clamped it to his ear… 'Talk to me… What's the situation? Okay… Got it…' He then hit another button and popped it back into his pocket before looking back to me…
'Seems we got a bit of a problem here, an acquaintance of ours made off with a substantial amount of money and it appears you were the last person to see him'
'I see a lot of people, perk of the trade, could you be a bit more specific?'

He sighed, rolled his eyes and clicked his fingers as one of the silent goons behind him stepped forward and handed him some photographs… He began sifting through them and pulled one out of the guy I'd killed and displayed it to me…

'Ring any bells with you Reggie? You don't mind if I call you Reggie do you?' he smirked. I played poker face but I don't mind admitting that it unsettled me that he knew my name.

'No, not at all… And no I ain't never seen him before'

Again he rolled his eyes, tutted and sighed as he flicked through more photographs 'til he found a blurry one of me bundling the guy into the back of my car and showed me…

'Ring any bells now Reggie?' he asked, tapping his finger on it… I was shocked he had photographs, we're normally so careful, it certainly gave me a lot to think about…

'Oh that guy? Can't say as I've seen him since, just drove him home to sleep off the booze…'

'Well that sounds all very chivalrous of you Reg, just one problem with that, call it the devil in the details if you will' he said, draping his arm around my shoulders in a comradely manner.

'What's that then?' I asked as innocently as possible.

'See the thing is, we had men at his place, waiting for him to retrieve the money but he never showed, we figured he'd fucked us over… But then we find that no one has heard hide nor hair of him since that day. Friends, family, business acquaintances, nada, zip, zilch, nothing…'

'Well I can see why that would trouble you, Friend'

'All roads lead back to you Reggie' he said, turning his comradely gesture into a head lock as he pulled a gun from his jacket and pressed it to my temple. 'And just for the record, I ain't your friend' he continued…

He then looked to the goons behind him. 'You three, get over to the house, Carlos said there's another guy in there, get him out here, just watch out for the dog' and off the three of them went over to the house.

Now I assume Carlos was the guy I'd seen driving into the other building earlier, the sneaky bastard had been watching us all along…

They were organized, I had to give them that… Somehow, I had to turn this around but I was fresh out of ideas and it was all happening too fast… I needed time to think…

A distraction maybe???

Next thing I know, there's a big crash, Jerry's barking his head off and there's a gun shot, then another and another… Jerry comes charging out of the house at the guy holding me, all bared teeth and growls… He quickly takes the gun from my head and shoots Jerry as he's about to pounce… Jerry went down with a yelp and the bastard actually laughed as he looked to his entourage with a smug grin 'And nobody else could've taken out the mutt??? What am I paying you guys for???' then they all laughed…

My heart sank and rage coursed through me as I swiftly dropped to my knee and punched upward hard, catching him square in the balls and took his gun as he went down, before training it on him… Suddenly there were four guns trained on me, each clicking in unison… But I knew they needed me so they weren't about to kill me… I kept the gun on him as he began to stand and two other goons returned from the house with Charles who looked pretty beaten up and had a gunshot wound to the shoulder…

His breathing was pretty shallow and his face was ashen, almost grey and sweaty… He was in shock and looked like he might pass out at any moment…

SHIT!!!

The leader of the pack then stepped forward, totally un-intimidated by me 'Come on, give it up Reggie… How do you think this is going to go down?' he smiled.
I looked at him through narrowed eyes and then briefly to Charles again. 'I think you are going to send him over to me and we're going to walk away, got it?' I growled.
The men all laughed, shifting on their feet as fingers itched over triggers… Their leader gestured for them all to calm down and be quiet.

'Its okay boys, humor him, let him have his fun' and they pushed Charles over to me as they lowered their guns…
That seemed a bit too easy… Charles staggered over to me, barely conscious…
'Come on Charles, this way, I'll get you out of here' I promised as the leader laughed.
'Touching ain't it boys? Sure does strum the heart strings don't it? Such heroics, such bravery, the cornerstone of friendships, I've got to say, I'm touched, I really am' he said with a slow deliberate clapping.
'Shut up!' I snapped. He then pointed at Charles as he got behind me.
'You've got to know I don't need him, don't you Reggie?' he said with a flick of the wrist of his pointing hand…

Suddenly, a gunshot echoed out from the adjacent building and Charles hit the floor as blood pumped out from the top of his head into the dirt, dead before he'd hit the ground…

FUCK!!!

I was seriously running out of options… I had to keep them talking and pray the girls didn't come back in the meantime… I hated to admit it but I think I'd found somebody who was more ruthless than I am…
And worse still, he had no concept of boundaries or compassion… The guy was a monster…

'Come on Reggie, how did you think this was going to play out? You've got to know we're not playing games here… You do know that, don't you Reggie? Now where is the money?' he said stepping closer to me.
'I don't know anything about the money, all I know is that prick came to my home and took my wife when he left… I let the fucker into my home and he runs off with my woman' I growled. He laughed, highly amused by the idea of this misfortune bestowed upon me.

'You poor, dumb bastard… You know, I actually believe you, always had a thing for the ladies that one… Almost makes me pity you, coz this ain't your day and your luck is not getting any better as time goes on… Things need to be rounded up but we seem to be at a bit of a stalemate… Carlos shoots you, you shoot me, there's probably balance in there somewhere but see, this is the thing, I'm not ready to go just yet'
'Then walk away'
'Ha, funny man… A very amusing concept but you know I can't do that, I can't leave until our business here is concluded'
'Well, I kind of had a feeling you'd say that but if you don't ask you don't get, right?'
'Very true…'

Another gunshot rang out from the adjacent building as one of the goons dropped to his knees then onto his face as his blood soaked into the dirt… The other men all looked around, spooked as a few more shots hit the ground around them, even catching one of them in the leg. He dropped and crawled for cover as all the others ran in different directions, guns drawn as they ducked behind cars and walls, waiting for the order or initiative for something or someone to shoot at…

I followed their lead and headed into the house out of the firing line… As the shooting stopped, the leader took out his phone and hit a button from his hiding place…
'Carlos? What the Hell are you playing at?'
'Carlos isn't here right now but if you'd like to leave a message I'll be sure to pass it on' crackled Tess' voice from Carlos' phone…

See, what I didn't find out 'til later was that Tess and Tish had heard the gunshots from further down the road on their way back from town, parked up and crept onto the industrial estate to see what was happening…
Tess was absolutely fuming when they shot Jerry and had to keep Tish from crying out when they shot Charles…
She'd then quickly headed to the building, found some shards of glass from a broken window, wrapped the thicker end of one with her head scarf so she could hold it without cutting herself, crept up behind Carlos and stabbed him hard in the throat. He shook, gargled and gasped as his blood pumped down his shirt from the wound. Then more so as she removed the shard and proceeded to slit his throat with it.

'Damn it, I've got blood all over my new dress' she griped, looking down at her blood soaked attire before looking to a shocked and freaked out Tish 'Don't you hate it when that happens?' she continued, shaking her head.

She then looked at Tish apologetically 'I'm so sorry, where are my manners? I should have let you do that... He's still just about alive if you'd like to finish him off or stab him a little' she said sincerely, offering the shard to Tish as he twitched and gasped beside her. Tish just shook her head quickly, her eyes full of fear and shock, waving her hand and stump in a desperate 'NO' gesture as tears streamed down her face.

'Are you sure? ...Oh too late... Sorry' she said with a sad smile as he twitched his last and lay still. Tish shook her head, clearly starting to lose it as she rambled...

'You're mad... Completely crazy... You stabbed him... You slit his throat... Then you offer me the weapon like it's the last muffin in the box... What's wrong with you? How can you do that? Well??? Answer me... What have you got to say for yourself?'

'Aren't you glad I'm on your side?' grinned Tess. Tish just shook her head disbelievingly as Tess picked up the gun and started taking shots into the yard until the bullets ran out and quickly answered Carlos' phone when it rang... She then reloaded the gun and began firing again...

In the meantime, I'd gotten into the house and quickly surveyed all the damage in there. One of the goons lay dead on the floor in the hallway, presumably shot by Charles before they'd dragged him outside 'Good for you, Charles... Good for you' I smiled sadly. He may have met his end but he'd taken one of the bastards down with him.

I had to wipe away a tear that threatened to cloud my sight, I was so proud of him but I'd have to grieve for both him and Jerry later when things had calmed down a bit... I found my gun discarded on the floor next to a pool of congealing blood... The goon's gun was still in his cold, dead hand, so I swiftly checked the corpse for ammo and filled my pockets...

I then picked up both guns and headed to the window as the gunfire started up again...

So where do we stand? Two dead on our side and three dead, one injured on their side...

See if we can't even up those odds a little... By my reckoning, there were still six of them and three of us... Though sadly I couldn't see Tish coping too well in an all out fire fight, so technically I guess it was just the two of us against the six of them...

I waited by the window as they all hid from Tess in Carlos' spot firing at them with them firing the occasional shots back... I think they'd all but forgotten about me in the excitement, which kind of makes them easy targets for me... I put one of the guns in my jacket pocket because as much as I'd love to tell you that I went Rambo on their arses, blazing in with a gun in each hand, I'm just really not that good a shot and needed to conserve the ammo... Besides, at this time, stealth was probably about my best weapon...

I could see the wounded goon hiding behind one of the cars taking pot shots at Tess, so I took aim, squeezed the trigger and took him out with a head shot without even having to break cover from the house... The others were out of my line of sight so I had to get out there...

I quickly made my way to the back of the house and out through the back door, figured I'd come at them from the other side and drive them into the maze of derelict cars…

As I reached the corner of the house and peeped around, there was one hiding behind the adjacent wall with his back to me… Too easy, I wouldn't even need the gun… So I picked up a crowbar that was leaning against the wall, crept up behind him, lifted it above my head and brought it crashing down on his scull, caveman style with as much force as I could muster… It was an interesting visual to say the least, his head all but split in two as it parted to a love heart shape to accommodate the crowbar's descent down its middle… He dropped, twitched and was still… I then took his gun and the ammo from his pockets before creeping away to the next one that came into sight…

He was hiding behind a car, so I crept up behind him, tapped him on the shoulder and pressed the gun up under his chin as he turned to face me… He froze and dropped his gun… If he was expecting mercy, I'm afraid I was all out of it, so I squeezed the trigger and blew the top of his head off in an explosion of blood, brain and scull fragments… It kind of put me in mind of some volcano footage I caught on the documentary channel a while back…

Interesting things, volcanoes, although that's not what you want to hear about right now is it? LMAO!!! Sorry, please pardon my laughing, but your face is a picture… Never have I seen anyone so avidly hooked on my words…

Now where was I? Oh yeah, I blew the top of his head off and he slumped, twitching beside the car… By my count, that was six of them dead and three left to go…

By this time I assumed Tess was out of ammo as her firing had ceased and I could see the goons were regrouping with the leader giving orders with a number of elaborate hand gestures… Including one that looked like he was pulling the chain of a toilet flush or train whistle… Most bizarre… But they seemed to understand and ran off in different directions out of my line of sight as the leader paced up and down as if in wait… Thankfully, I still had the element of surprise from my vantage point behind him… So I just kept an eye on him and began to take aim with the gun…

Tess meanwhile, having run out of ammo at the adjacent building had begun to make her way to the yard with Tish in toe… One of the goons had spotted them and quickly pursued them, waiting behind the gate as they approached… As the first to enter, he'd grabbed Tess as she'd passed him, jamming the gun against her head… His mistake really… As soon as he moved the gun away to cover Tish, Tess pulled the shard of glass from the folds of her dress, turned and slid it effortlessly up under his ribcage to his shock and surprise as blood poured over her hands as she twisted it, pulled it out and quickly slit his throat as he dropped to his knees and fell face first into the dirt…

'OH GOD… OH GOD… OH GOD…' repeated Tish, clearly freaking out again as Tess relieved the corpse of its gun and ammo… Sadly Tish's freaking out was short-lived as the other goon appeared from the side of the house and shot her outright in the head. She dropped without a sound as the gunshot echoed in the air. He turned to cover Tess as she ran to Tish and dropped to her knees beside her as tears welled up in her eyes. 'Drop the gun and don't do anything stupid' he barked at her. She did as she was told and raised her arms as she got to her feet resignedly.

'Now move' he continued, displaying the way with a nodding gesture of his gun. Unlike the previous goon, this one was careful to keep her five feet in front of him as he marched her away.

As I was just about to pull the trigger on the leader, I saw Tess being marched in by the remaining goon and relief washed over me that she hadn't been the focus of the gunshot I'd heard... But my relief soon turned to sorrow as I realized Tish wasn't with them coz I know Tess would have kept her with her... My fear was confirmed by the redness of Tess' eyes and the tears on her cheeks... Tish too was dead...

The leader grinned triumphantly and threw car keys to the goon 'Go get the car started, we're nearly done here' he said confidently 'Yes Boss' came the reply and off the goon went... The Leader then strode up and gripped Tess roughly by the hair, pressed his gun into her temple and dragged her into view...
'Reggie, get out here... I've got your woman... I know you're watching... Come on... I'm going to give you to the count of five, then I'm going to shoot her... You hear me?'
I froze for a moment, I honestly didn't know what to do...
I'd lost too much that day, I couldn't risk losing Tess too...
But he had positioned her to block my shot, I felt helpless.
'One...'
'Don't listen to him Reg' said Tess defiantly.
'Two...'
'Shoot him Reg'
'Three'
'Kill the Fucker'
'Four'

Tess scrunched her eyes shut and I quickly stepped out of my hiding place…

'STOP!!! Don't hurt her… Please' I pleaded.

'Aww Reggie, you're breaking my heart, you noble bastard' he laughed. 'But you've got to know we only need one of you, you do know that, right?' He asked, grinning.

And as he raised his gun arm to shoot me, three things happened in quick succession, Tess went mad and threw off his aim as she bucked, I instinctively jumped back as the gun went off, tripped and banged my head on the wall beside me which knocked me unconscious and Tess, seeing me fall went feral, thinking I'd been shot and launched herself at the leader, biting deeply into his throat, blood pumping out over her face as she tore out his larynx with her bare teeth… That's my girl…

By this time, like I say, I was unconscious but as I'm told, he'd dropped to the floor with a terrified, shocked look on his face as the remaining goon came back in to see what was happening… He saw me and must have assumed the same as Tess, that I was dead. He then hit Tess over the back of the head with butt of his gun as she was finishing up with the leader… Then carried her out to the car, stashed her in the trunk and drove away…

I awoke a little while later, saw the leader and then panicked… Where was Tess? I quickly went over to his body and searched his pockets for some clue as to where they would have taken her… I pulled out a number of business cards for the bar where it had all began so many months earlier with the date rapist… Things were so much simpler then… I felt like I'd lost everything, my friends, my lover and my dog…

They were my life and now they were all gone… I didn't know what to do, my world had fallen apart around me and there was nothing I could do about it…

There were bodies all over the yard and in the house, so I couldn't even call the police and report her abduction without a lot of awkward questions, potential arrest and maybe even prison time by the time the police were through combing the area for clues… I knew I had to take the fight to them… In my favor, they thought I was dead so they wouldn't see it coming… And if there was a chance Tess was still alive, I had to go after her… But I'm just one man… When did my life become so complicated?

Well Friend, I'll have to tell you more next time…
Sorry to keep you hanging but I've got things to do and time is creeping on…

You have a great day now…

And thanks for listening…

Dark Confessions
...For Love, Honor & Glory...

Well here we are again…

Good to see you as always Friend…

I apologize if I may have come across as a bit maudlin last time we spoke but I'm still coming to terms with it all… It was such a hard time, I'd lost so much in the space of a day and there was no time to grieve… I had to strategize attack plans and the yard was full of bodies, I prayed that no customer's would come 'til I'd gotten the place straightened out… Strangely enough, nobody did but I found out later that day why that was…

See, one thing you can say for the mob, is they know how to clean up after themselves… I remember seeing three black vans coming up the dirt road and in truth I panicked… I honestly thought they were the police, figured it was game over and the fat lady was most assuredly singing… So I'd grabbed a large bag of food, the money and all the guns I'd collected, headed up to the attic and kept an eye on things through the attic window that overlooked the yard… After all, I didn't know how long I was going to be up there or if it came to it, if I'd have to shoot my way out…

Thankfully, it didn't come to that eventuality, they parked up the vans and about twenty guys in what looked like hazmat suits filed out and set to work… My heart sank when I saw the hazmat suits, figured they were forensics, combing the area for evidence of foul play… But there were no police detectives hanging about and not so much as a blue light, siren or box of doughnuts to herald their arrival… Clearly they were a mob clean up crew and in fairness, were doing a bang up job…

In fact I'd go as far as to say, I was impressed by their efficiency as they collected and wrapped all the bodies, washed away all signs of blood, fixed up the windows and doors and within two hours, you couldn't even tell anything untoward had happened there... Absolutely incredible...

They even had someone to take over the running of the yard in the belief that I was one of the dead... I guess an old scrap yard on an abandoned industrial estate makes for a good shop front when dealing with stolen cars, known cars and even makes for a good base of operations... Like fuck was I going to let them take away my yard, been there all my life, it was my livelihood...

I waited for all the vans to leave and started to formulate a plan as I watched my would be replacement stroll around the yard, getting to grips with the layout and equipment... I don't mind telling you I was pretty pissed off by this time, I mean, how much did they think they were going to take from me? But I knew I had to keep a cool head, one mistake and that would be my arse... First things first, I had to take care of this prick who thought he was having my yard... I realize he was probably in constant contact with this Mikey guy, a new investment or ill gotten property would have to be watched and nurtured for kinks in its running...

I had to get off the property without the guy seeing me, which was easier said than done... So while he has strolling around the yard, I came down from the attic, nipped out to the stock shed when I saw he was over by the crusher... 'Stock shed at a junk yard?' I hear you ask incredulously...

We actually sold a full range of car and household tools, tool kits, torches and knives with attached tools and some even had built in mini-torches… They sold quite well coz as we all know, guys love their gadgets and toys…

Anyway, I headed to and opened a box of original 'Swiss Army knives' (Still one of our most popular sale items), took out four and popped them into my pockets…
I then checked to see the coast was clear and headed back to the house… I took the 'Rohypnol' out of the cupboard, emptied two out of the bottle into my hand before returning them to the cupboard and cautiously awaited his return…

About twenty minutes later, he came in, filled and turned on the kettle and set himself up a cup with a tea bag in it and then tucked into one of my frosted muffins out of the fridge… Cheeky fucker…

As the kettle finally rumbled to the boil, he poured the water into the cup and left it stand while he nipped off to the toilet… Perfect…
I took the opportunity to pop the 'Rohypnol' into his tea and quietly stirred it before creeping outside to wait for him to nod off…

After about half an hour had passed, I crept up to the window, peeped in and smiled… He was flat out in **MY** chair in front of **MY** T.V… So I nipped back in and changed my clothes upstairs, figured the blood splats might look a bit conspicuous… I favored my black clothes to match my mood and maybe subconsciously as a statement of mourning for those that I'd lost that day…

Shirt, jeans, boots and my long coat to conceal all the guns and topped it off with my hoodie top so I wouldn't be instantly recognizable to any security cameras… I put a small slit in the lining of the coat, lined up with each pocket and popped the 'Swiss Army Knives' in… Two in the left and two in the right and let them drop to the bottom of coat…

I then filled every pocket with the collection of guns I'd acquired earlier that day along with the ammo… Pretty much ready to go, so I popped on my shades and looked myself over in the mirror… Then topped it off with my black gloves… I didn't look much like me but I've got to say, I looked pretty damn cool… I then loaded up my back pack, with a hacksaw, wire cutters and a change of clothes for Tess (She was pretty bloodied when they took her)…

I was still pretty steamed about this guy moving into my house and yard so as my last act of defiance before I left, I sprinkled a soft layer of fiber-glass dust over the top of the remaining frosted muffins… Judging by the way he wolfed down the last one, I imagine he will have eaten half of it before he realizes its cutting his throat to pieces from the inside… Oh to be a fly on the wall when he discovers that, later… LMAO!!! Figured I could clear the body away when I got back…

I looked around outside and realized I couldn't use his car or he'd notice it gone when he woke up…
Then it suddenly occurred to me that Tess and Tish must have parked up further down the dirt road to avoid being seen when they heard the gunshots… So I headed off down the road on foot and smiled when our car came into view about a quarter of a mile away from the yard…

I ran the rest of the way to the car and found the keys under the front tyre and swiftly jumped into the driving seat... That's my girl...

I found her gloves appropriately in the glove box and put them in my pocket, I then quickly gunned the engine and was on my way into town...

I happened to notice on my way off the dirt road that there was a sign, warning of a hazardous chemical spill and to turn back... Certainly explains why no customers had been to the yard since the goons arrived... They probably would have thought the gunshots were chemical explosions... You've got to give credit where it's due in the extent they go to cover their tracks, no stone is left unturned...

I quickly stopped off at the garden center and bought ten large sacks of weed killer... It was to be my back up plan, you see weed killer has a delightfully explosive chemical in it called 'Sodium Chlorate'... I remember seeing a documentary a long while back that told of its use for making bombs in the Second World War and even how modern day terrorists were making use of it... My logic was 'If Tess was dead, I'd use the car as a bomb and drive it into the bar and detonate it'...

Now I realize that may sound a bit drastic but without Tess, Jerry, Charles and Tish, I had very little left to lose and even less to live for... And I wasn't going down without a fight, I was taking those bastards with me... But I won't dwell on that now, suffice to say, it was plan B...

Plan A was in motion, I was heading to the bar, locked and loaded... I knew there wasn't any point in marching in through the front door, too public...

So I drove the car around the back to the delivery area and parked up next to the loading bay and found a way in through the beer cellar… It was just a quick snip with the wire cutters on the chain that secured the door and I was in… Again stealth was my best weapon, they didn't know I was there…

The first goon I came across stood in a doorway with his back to me… I had the bright idea that I would break his neck like they do in the movies, I'd never done it before but it always looked easy enough… Get behind them, sharp twist, crack, down they go without any fuss… Sounds simple huh? The reality… I crept up behind him, tried to crack his neck, he cried out and fell backwards, holding his neck in pain… Obviously some technique I'm missing… He saw me, went for his gun, so I punched him hard in the face and he toppled over…

As he hit the ground, I swiftly kicked his head like a football and repeatedly stamped on his throat 'til with a final crack, he was still… Certainly got my heart racing… That could have gone so horribly wrong…

I then dragged him into a corner and put a sheet of tarpaulin over him that had previously been covering some barrels… I didn't even see the second goon, he charged at me as I was covering up the first one, knocking me to the floor… I quickly rolled over and kicked his legs out from under him as he went for his gun and I was on him as he hit the floor… I the quickly reached over my shoulder, pulled the hacksaw out of my bag and brought it across his throat in one fluid movement… The teeth tearing sharply and briefly over his jugular as blood pumped out over his neck…

He choked, gargled and gasped as his hands scrabbled at his neck 'til his eyes rolled upward and he twitched 'til he was still… I swiftly put him with the other goon's corpse and covered them both with the tarpaulin…

The hacksaw was a bloody mess so I left it there under the gas boiler lest Tess's clean clothes be as bad as the ones she was wearing… I then headed out of the cellar, there were two sets of stairs, one by my calculations led to the bar area, the other into the staff area… So I went with the latter, up the stairs beyond the passage way and into a corridor that displayed a lot of doors, so I began to snoop around…
And then they came…

Now this time, I did have a gun in each hand and fired as each door opened… Taking them down, one by one, dropping empty guns as I pulled loaded ones from my pockets… It was a blood bath and I was as cool as fuck, even if I do say so myself… I had no fear and nothing to lose… By Hell or high water, I would find Tess or die in the trying… And so on I trod without breaking step as yet more bodies fell in my wake…
Although in truth, I must confess that the high kill rate in my 'Matrix' style rampage probably had more to do with the close proximity of the narrow corridor and the element of surprise than any skill or talent I might have possessed with the guns…

Everything was going great until one of the goons got a lucky shot in and caught me in the shoulder… I took him out with my next shot and ducked into a side room with a sharp intake of breath and a wince as I felt the bite of the bullet wound…

Luckily, I think it was just a flesh wound as the bullet passed straight through without any bone damage…

…Still hurt like a bastard though…

Sadly, as I got inside and closed the door behind me, fifteen guns suddenly clicked in unison and as I turned, I found myself staring down their barrels as I discovered them all aimed directly at me…

OH CRAP!!!

I quickly dropped the guns I was holding and raised my hands, despite the pain it caused me… In fact it was fucking agony but I didn't want to give them the satisfaction of knowing that…

'STOP!' a gruff voice barked behind them… They then lowered their weapons and two of them stepped forward, took my back pack and began roughly patting me down and emptying my pockets of the remaining guns and ammo 'til I stood before them weaponless… 'You must be Reggie I take it, we've been expecting you…' continued the gruff voice as the goons parted to allow the voice's owner through… He was a guy in his late forties, slightly overweight with silver streaked hair and a face like a leather handbag… 'And you must be Mikey' I replied as he shook my hand before one of the goons returned my back pack…

'Whatta you know? My reputation precedes me' he laughed, looking around at his goons who returned the laugh at his cue… 'I gotta say Reg, you certainly know how to make an entrance' he smiled.

'It's a gift, I was always brought up to believe first impressions count' I retorted sarcastically…

'Wise sentiment' he chuckled and embraced me, wrapping both his arms around my shoulders before kissing me on each cheek, almost fondly before continuing.

'You know, I like you Reggie, you and your good lady have caused me a lot of trouble. Between taking out some of my best men at your yard and now blasting your way through here like the Terminator, I should be as mad as Hell… But I've got to say, I'm impressed… Not many would have the balls to pull the shit you have, it shows passion and strength, I respect that'
'Thanks… I think…' I frowned…
'See, we didn't see any potential threat at the yard, we figured it would be run of the mill, owned by 'Johnnie Nobody'… Get in there, get the money and get rid of the witnesses… A quick, clean job… No mess, no fuss, easy money…'
'I'm sorry to disappoint you'
'Oh I'm not disappointed, far from it… It fair made my day, excitement, action, drama… I was literally on the edge of my seat with each update about the operation, my heart hasn't beat like that in years. I even had to pop a few blood pressure pills… Fantastic… And now here you are in the flesh like a one man army'
I just came here for Tess and then I'll be out of your hair'
'There's no need to be in such a rush, Tess is fine… She's a feisty little thing isn't she? She's killed two of my men since she's been here' he laughed. 'I know she'll be overjoyed to see you, she didn't believe us when we told her you were still alive, hence she killed the two guys guarding her…'
'How did you know I was still alive?'

'Your body didn't show up with the rest of them from the yard, I figured you'd be coming. I just didn't expect you so soon.'

'Yeah, that was kind of the idea'

'See, this is what I like about you Reggie, you're impulsive, resourceful, unpredictable and maybe even a little reckless but you show such huge potential and promise'

'I don't understand…'

'I'd like you and Tess to come and work for me, I'd be proud to have you both on the payroll'

'I'm afraid I'm really not much of a people person'

'I'll even forget the million and pay you by the job, what do say Reg?'

'I'll have to think on it, at the moment I just want to see Tess'

'Well of course, I'll take you to her now… ' he said gesturing the door jovially. 'And Reggie, don't think on it too long…' he continued with a hint of menace in his voice.

He led me along a corridor to another room where Tess would be waiting… I mean, in truth, it had really given me a lot to think about… If I said yes, we could go home without any worry of retaliation; we could keep the million and just be called in for the occasional unsavory job with a pay packet… Tempting huh? But then we have to consider Jerry, Charles and Tish, did he think I was just going to forget about them and play happy soldier? And these jobs he talks of, they'll be decent people who dared to say no… That kind of goes against the grain for me, I've only ever killed scum and I can justify that to myself…

But decent ordinary people? I don't think I'd be able to look at myself in the mirror each day… There was no question about it; me and Tess were just going to have to get out of there and to Hell with the consequences…

Although I hadn't realized quite how high the price of those consequences would be… You see, I love Tess so very much; I would do anything for that woman… I would go to Hell and back… I would die for her… And I don't say that lightly, I mean it with all my heart…

I'm sorry Friend, but I'm afraid I'm going to have to leave it there for now… And I apologize for leaving you hanging again, but I promise I'll finish the story next time… Honest…

You have a nice day now…

Thanks for listening…

Dark Confessions
...Sacrifice, Fury & Vengeance...

Here we are again Friend, just as I promised…

I'm so sorry I've been having to go at the most inopportune moments, but just telling you about this stuff is really hard for me… But it's like I said before, I'm still coming to terms with it all… I'd lost so much and I stood to lose so much more… Please bare with me, I'm trying…

Now where was I? Oh yeah, Mikey had made me a proposition but I knew in my heart that I couldn't accept it… It was more than my conscience would allow… But I also knew that if we'd said no, they'd have killed us both without a second thought… So as you can imagine, it was a tricky situation… Damned if we do, dead if we don't… In fact the only light at the end of the tunnel for me at this time was they were going to reunite me with Tess…

In the distance, I could hear approaching police sirens, obviously in response to the sound of gun fire. A bit of a worry me thinks… Finally we reached the room Tess was being kept in and he opened the door for me to enter… The first thing I saw was Tess' fist as it impacted my face… Bloody typical… I'd marched in there, leaving a trail of carnage without so much as a scratch 'til that bullet caught me, then within a second of seeing Tess, the damn woman breaks my nose… Ironic really, that I'd come here to save her… I mean yeah, she is a crazy bitch but she's my crazy bitch and I love her to death… She just stopped herself landing a kick to my balls as she realized it was me… Her mouth did a perfect 'O' as she quickly covered it with her hands… 'Oh Reggie, I'm so sorry' she said as I tasted blood… She then got hyper excited and hugged me 'REGGIE!!!' she cried, kissing me.

'I'll leave you love birds to catch up' said Mikey with a laugh as a goon approached him…

'Mikey, the police are here about the gun shots'

He just shook his head as I looked at him 'Don't worry Reggie, I'll soon send them on their way' he said with a smile as he left, leaving one of the goons to shut and lock the door…

Clearly they'd let Tess wash all the blood from her face and hands but she still wore the blood soaked clothes, so I gave her the clean ones out of the back pack and she put them to one side for a moment…

'Are you okay Reggie?' she asked, kissing me again…

'I'll live…' I smiled 'I'm just so happy to see you, I feared the worst'

'So did I, I thought you were dead, I didn't think I'd ever see you again… I love you so much' she said looking deep into my eyes as I stroked her cheek…

'I love you too…' I replied and kissed her…

We then just hugged for a moment, so relieved that we were back together, then we caught up with everything we'd been through since we last saw each other and she started fussing about the bullet wound in my shoulder…

She then tutted and shook her head in mock indignation…

'Oh you big baby, there's not even any bone damage and the bullet went straight through' she said rolling her eyes with a grin… 'We'll soon numb that for you' she then pulled out a bag of white powder, tore open the top and patted some on the entry and exit wounds…

'What's that?' I asked.

'Mob cocaine, 100% pure, I think one of the guards I killed was due to deliver it somewhere, I swiped it from his coat before they took the body away' she winked.

'Thanks… I think…' I laughed. And fair dues, it did numb the area nicely… 'Right we have to work out how we're going to get out of here' I said, getting down to business as she changed into the clean clothes.

'I've been thinking on that and I do have a way of getting out of this room, but we don't have any weapons to get us any further'

'I think I can help out with that' I said, feeling for the 'Swiss Army Knives' in the bottom of my coat lining. I then opened one of the blades through the lining and used it to cut a hole from within and extracted them…

'Swiss Army Knives? You're kidding me' she laughed incredulously…

'Trust me, I know what I'm doing'

I then opened the two blades either end of the knife and pulled open the spiky bit on the other side…

I demonstrated the concept, by placing the knife in my palm and gripped it to make a fist with the spike sticking out between my second and third fingers, mid fist at the knuckle and the blades either side of the fist with the option to stab up or down… I then took my gloves and made the appropriate slits within for the blades and spike…

When I was done and the knife inside, I did the same to my other glove and put them on to show her, pulling a mock 'Wolverine' pose which made her giggle…

'Aww… I want a pair…' she said excitedly…

'Ask and you shall have my dear' I winked and pulled her gloves out of my pocket and did the same to them with the other two 'Swiss Army Knives'…

'Pretty' she said as she tried them on excitedly and did a twirl 'Do they go with my outfit?' she joked. I laughed

'Very sexy, you look adorable' I said wiggling my eyebrows. 'Okay my dear, your turn… It's time we left' I continued, getting back to business…

'Time to shine, huh?' she smiled and went to a cupboard in the corner of the room and took out a box of shotgun shells…
'I guess they thought ammunition would be useless without the weapons to fire them' she winked. 'I saw this in a film called 'Phantasm' years ago' she continued. She then proceeded to take a drawing pin from a cork board on the wall and pushed it into the top of the shell, took a hammer and a roll of masking tape from the cupboard and taped the shell to the hammers head… 'Are you ready lover' she said with a sexy smile, holding the hammer aloft like some foxy, female Thor…
'Just one thing before we go' I said.
'What's that then?'
'A kiss of your soft lips to sustain me through the coming storm, my love' I said. Smooth huh?
'Ooh Reggie, when did you start getting poetic? I like it' she replied, embracing me as we kissed passionately…

Then just as she was about to swing the hammer at the lock, we heard the door unlock from the other side so she quickly hid it behind her back…
She looked at me and shrugged as two goons came into the room and then swung the hammer regardless at the first one's head… Head and shell exploded on impact in a loud blast of fire, blood, brains and scull that echoed through the building, taking out the goon behind him too… We looked at each other stunned, we SO hadn't been expecting that to happen… So much for a quiet exit…

She quickly dropped the hammer and we swiftly stepped over the bodies as they fell, made our way into the corridor and began running… At first, we seemed to have a clean break but then they started coming… Tess took out the first with an upper cut that sent the spike of the glove in under his chin and twisted the punch so the side blade slit his throat as she pulled it out…

I took out the next with spiked punch to the forehead… The third grabbed Tess from behind, she quickly stamped on his toe, twisted around and stabbed him in the eye with a punch… As he cried out, she crashed her fists together, either side of his head, the blades sinking forcefully into his temples… The next was mine as I first stabbed him in the chest with a spike punch, then slit his throat before he could cry out and he dropped twitching at my feet…

We then stooped to take the guns and ammo from the fallen goons… I mean the gloves were effective and incredibly efficient for close proximity fighting but very soon we'd be likely to hit goons with the shooting distance to take us down… It was time for us to take up arms and shoot our way out… And that's exactly what we did as guns blazed on both sides with as many misses as hits and a few close calls along the way for us too…

Finally, we'd hit the cellar where I'd come in and immediately got jumped by three goons… One of them punched Tess in the mouth and she went down, quickly grabbing the hacksaw I'd left there earlier by the gas boiler… Another kicked me hard in the back and sent me flying across the room and I felt the crash as my face impacted something made of glass and felt a broken shard slice into my cheek as I passed through it… I sucked air in through my teeth as I pulled my head out of the fire axe case I'd collided into…

Tess meanwhile, brought the hacksaw in a smooth arc across the neck of the goon who'd punched her as he came charging toward her, his blood trailing the saw's trajectory as he dropped to his knees and then onto his face…
Still dazed, I began to get up and grabbed hold of the fire axe to help me stand without realizing what it was… Then I did… And as the goon ran at me, I pulled the axe from its case and swiftly brought it crashing down on his head… It seemed to happen in slow motion as I grabbed the axe and immediately began the swing as it left the casing, he looked up to see it coming down at him but was to late to retreat as his momentum continued to carry him toward me, I saw the fear and realization in his eyes just as the axe split his head in two and he dropped twitching at my feet…
The third went after Tess and she kicked him hard into the wall beside me… I swung a quick horizontal arc with the axe and decapitated his head at the neck as his body slid down the wall, his head bouncing twice before rolling into the corner…

'Are you okay?' I asked, kissing her…
'I'm fine Reg' she smiled 'How is your shoulder?'
'Aching but I'll cope… Right, you go out to the car and get it started, the keys are already in the ignition'
'Okay, what are you going to do?'
'I've got an axe and there are gas pipes here, what do you think I'm going to do?' I laughed. She smiled.
'Okay, don't be long… I love you'
'I love you too… I'll be right behind you'
We kissed and she quickly left through the door to the loading bay and our waiting car…

I then quickly used the axe to chop into the gas pipes, carefully making sure not to hit the wall behind for fear of sparks… Then holding my breath, I bent the severed pipe ends outward to quicker fill the cellar with gas…

I figured if any more goons entered the cellar after us and smelt the gas or saw the pipes, it would add as a great distraction when they called upstairs and it may even stop them firing their guns for fear of igniting it… A far stretch I know but I was trying every angle I could think of in our bid to get away… And trust me, they weren't making it easy for us… I then got out after Tess…

'REGGIE! HURRY UP…' she called from the car 'THERE'S MORE OF THEM COMING…' she continued as more goons began appearing at the gate we were due to exit from…

I quickly got in and she hit the gas peddle hard, wheel spinning us into motion to a hail of gun fire at the gate… The windows exploded around us as she ploughed through the goons… And with much relief I actually thought for a moment we were home and dry as we sped off down the road, getting a fair distance without pursuit… I kept a vigilant look through the back window until without warning, Tess slumped over the wheel and we careened into some garbage bins with a crash as they erupted rubbish into the air around us… 'TESS' I cried out as the car came to a stop…

She looked up at me drowsily, spitting blood from her beautiful lips… 'I'm sorry…' she whispered with tears in her eyes…

'No, no, don't be sorry… You got us out of there Tess…' I said leaning toward her and stroking her cheek in concern… I then managed to get her to sit up straighter and checked her wound… It looked like a bullet had caught her in the chest, left lung, I'd say if I was looking at it right… 'Oh Tess… Baby…' I said cradling her and kissing her forehead with trembling lips 'Don't you dare leave me' I continued, blinking away tears that were forming in my eyes… Her skin was becoming pale and clammy, not a good sign… 'I'm not going to make it Reggie… Take the money and start a new life… Just promise me, you won't forget me…'

'Don't talk like that Tess… I'm not going anywhere without you… I'd die first…'

I quickly went to the trunk and pulled out a first aid kit, patching her up as best as I could to stop the bleeding… She was drowsy and slipping in and out of consciousness but with her help, I moved her over to the passenger seat and kept her talking…

It was breaking my heart, I knew she wasn't going to make it… And it was tearing me apart that she knew it too…

Those bastards were going to pay… BIG TIME!!!

I got into the driving seat and slammed the car into reverse, turned around and headed back to the bar…

…Plan B it was then…

About half an hour had passed since we had initially left the bar so I think it was safe to assume that they would think we wouldn't be back by choice…

So as soon as the bar came into view I made sure both Tess and I were buckled into our seats… After all, safety first… I then hit the accelerator peddle to the max and aimed the car at the bar's front doors, crashing through them and skidding inside as I took out some tables and goons 'til I swung the car to a stop as staff ran for the exit…

I then popped open the trunk so the sacks of weed killer were easily accessible to flame… I leapt out of the car over the bar, killed the barman as I grabbed his hair and repeatedly smashed his face into the counter top, then started smashing all the spirit bottles and pouring others to make a flammable, alcoholic trail to the car… I then leapt over the bar to the cellar door and kicked it open… The gas smell that hit me was overpowering… I coughed and shook my head to clear it as I took my Zippo lighter from my pocket and headed back to the car…

'REGGIE… STOP!!!' I heard Mikey call from the other side of the room… 'We can talk about this…'
'I'm done talking Mikey, I have nothing left to talk about'
'But this is madness, everybody loses…'
'Well I've already lost everything, so we'll call it a draw'
Two of his goons took out their guns and pointed them at me. Mikey looked absolutely horrified…
'Not a very persuasive argument guys, one spark and you do my job for me' I grinned.
'He's right, put the guns away you fucking idiots' added Mikey with a growl. They sheepishly did as they were told and he covered his mouth with a hanky as the gas continued to fill the room… 'Reggie, please… Think about this, it's not worth it… We can make a deal…'
'I'm done with deals… Now if you'll excuse me I have to check on Tess, she's dying you know…'

'Then let me get a doctor in here, we might be able to save her'

'And how would that work Mikey? I'd be indebted to you? I don't think so' I said and coughed… It was then that I realized what he was doing… The prick was keeping me talking, hoping I'd pass out as the air to gas ratio was shifting into oxygen starvation… Clever bastard…

I then got back into the car to see how Tess was… Not good… She weakly smiled and put her arms around my shoulders…

'Do it Reggie… But tell me you love me one last time…'

'I love you so much Tess, you are my world…'

'And I love you Reggie… I just needed to hear it one more time… Now kiss me…'

And so we kissed for the last time…

A kiss that ended our world in flame by the fire of its passion as I used my thumb to flick the top off the Zippo and strike its flint… It sparked, igniting the air around us, roared as it hit the spirits at the bar and boomed as it hit the weed killer in the trunk, killing everyone in a fire ball that belched and crashed out of every window and door in the building…

Dark Confessions
…The Last Confession…

Hey Friend,

You probably won't remember writing this, so just read it and add it to the narrative… I've taken the driving seat for a while to conclude my thoughts and speak more directly to you… I'm not sure how that works but it does so I'm not asking any questions and I'm running with it… After all, why fix what's not broken?

Now I realize you are probably wondering how the Hell to finish the story with your main character dead yet maintain the continuity of having him speak a first person narrative in the past tense… Am I right? What do you want me to say? I'm dead? I've passed over? I lost my life in a blaze of glory? Call it what you will, it makes no odds to me… I'm just happy you've been writing it all down, it means a lot to me…

See the thing is Fritz… I hope you don't mind me calling you Fritz… I needed someone to tell my story and it means a lot to me that it was you… It doesn't matter to me whether you perceive me as a symptom of your own madness, a voice in your head or a lost soul looking for absolution… Nor do I care if you believe me or not… Admittedly, I may have exaggerated a little here and there but who doesn't when they have a rapt audience…

Like I told you before, I like your work, its unique and engaging, your book **'Fear the Reaper'** with its first person narrative lent such intensity to the piece that I knew it had to be you who told my tale… I had to take the chance that all the voices within you aren't your own and I was right…

You heard me and you wrote my **"Dark Confessions"** with such clarity and intensity that I am moved beyond words…

And even you have to admit you've enjoyed the ride for all its thrills, chills and twists and you have a great story to show for it…

But it's not for me to take credit or glorify in the events, I simply had to unburden myself of my sins in life… This is my gift to you as your story telling is your gift to me…

I needed to be heard one last time as much as I needed to speak the words aloud… And your gift has allowed me do just that and for that I am eternally grateful…

Thank you so much…

Just remember, not all the stories come from within, they're all around you, you just have to listen… And like me, they're desperate to be heard and eager to be told, so just be receptive and they will come…

Have a great day now…

And thank you for listening…

All the best,

Your friend,

Reggie……….

Bonus Chapter

-Dark Impulses-

...Poetic Murder & Ascending Contemplations...

As featured in "Touching the Darkness"

A Symphony of Dark Desires

A divine symphony
of archaic pleasures
doth release the
Beast within…
Effervescent thoughts
disperse in dark clouds
behind mine eyes
as a veil of condensation
glazes my pupils…

I bite gleefully
into an over ripe plum
and wipe'th away
its rust colored deposit
from my chin…

Mine heart-beat
doth quicken
as I dost see her,
consuming me
with a blood lust
that doth chill me
to my bones…

Unbidden thoughts
doth slither
amidst cascading
dreamscapes,
like a serpent in Eden…
Tempting me…
Taunting me…
Playing with me…

The evening's humid heat
overwhelms my senses…
I need air…
I need to think…
I need to dispel
these wrongful thoughts…
Why dost this virgin bride
fill'eth me with such
awful desires?

Its like a disease…
So primal…
So sexual in nature…
Wouldst I truly sacrifice
everything in my life?
Just to let my demon rise
beneath a moonless sky
and sate his need?

He is very perceptive…
He awakens
and is lucid in my mind…
He softly whispers
his deviancy
to mine open ears,
causing me to blush
and salivate in rapture
at my moral decline…

He drives me…
Controls me like a machine
of most unholy intent…
And so I am lost…
Engulfed by my darkness
in a maelstrom of voices
as my very sanity ebbs
into a cold, empty void…
Beyond hope…
Beyond reason…
Beyond salvation…

I smile to see that she has joined me…

<u>The Room</u>

I return after so many years,
awaiting remembrance
to breach my lost past.
A cold unease consumes me,
as voices of forgotten ghosts
whisper softly to my senses…
Teasing my perceptions
with forsaken illusions…

Children playing, laughter,
music, the smell of fresh bread…
Such pleasant memories are these,
so why is my mind bestowing
this ill feeling dread upon me?
Numbness consumes my soul
from the very core of my being.
What happened here?

A scream, tearing flesh,
splash of blood, open wounds…
Moaning, hissing, crying…
What is this?
Temples pounding… Racing heart,
fingernails digging
into sweaty palms,
drawing bloody half moons…

The chair stands empty,
foreboding, familiar,
amidst unfolding memories
of lost dreams in an empty room…
Hooks, pain, blood, a cry…
Light bulb swinging, shadows swaying,
laughter, a voice… my voice…
my mind… my alter ego…

Welcome Home!!!

Death Art

Day to day, finding prey,
To hunt when night doth fall.
Find the one, thy will be done,
And so my demons call.
Racing heart, a beat apart,
As lust for blood ensues.
So I crave, to misbehave,
The taste of fear, my muse.

So tonight, beneath lamp light,
Heels on concrete ring.
Hold my breath, for twilight death,
And all the pain I'll bring.
Now I stalk as prey doth walk,
Unknown to what's in store.
Looking round at every sound,
This primal fear so raw.

So turned on, I lust and long,
And strike from shadows cold.
Fearing eyes that question why,
Recoiling from my hold.
Fear thee not, thy fear begot,
The best is yet to come.
In my reign, I'll show you pain,
Before your senses numb.

In my heart, my work is art,
And she, my canvas bare.
Cut her deep, and make her weep,
And whimper as I stare.
Cutting lines as art defines,
With patterns crimson red,
Bleed her dry and bid goodbye,
Before her body's dead.

Passion quelled, where life once dwelled,
And now to bleach her skin.
Take away, my marks of play,
And wash away my sin.
Quickly ferried, corpse is buried,
Under basement floor.
So I weep, before I sleep,
And pray there are no more…

God Complex

I may have been born of you,
but I am not one of you…
You sicken me, repulse me
with your abhorrent nature.
Self serving, paranoid,
territorial primitives,
serving the superficial,
worshipping the veneer
in vanity and self indulgence
in worthless lives
that amount to naught
but chaos in the turmoil of your flaws,
forever fighting in a world
that has not seen a day without war
since your creation…

I am the loner that does not fit in,
I am the truth that you ignore,
I am the conscience that you bury
in justification of your actions,
I am the justice from which you hide,
I am the darkness and the light,
I bring order to chaos,
I am the cure to this blight called humanity,
this scourge of the Earth's misery,
I am the man who would destroy the world…

And so I hear you laugh,
well lap it up my friend
'cause I'm top of the fucking food chain
and I'll be dabbing up your gravy
as I pick your chunks from my teeth.
You see, what you don't know doesn't hurt you,
blissful ignorance of imminent demise
allows you to carry on infesting
a dying world that begs its end.
And I will bring its end…

International waters, no law, no problem.
Your rules, your law, your game.
Drilling depths, punching crust,
penetrating layers of time
to drain a polluted ocean into a molten core,
building leagues of steam to fatal pressure
and so the planet tears itself apart.
You do the math, end of days,
End of the world,
Game over, Checkmate!!!
Eternity beckons…

You don't know
how long I've been doing it,
how close I am or even if I've started.
Why don't you sleep on it
and tell me how you feel
in the morning,
if indeed
there is a morning…

Who's laughing now???

Temperance and Gluttony (7 form)

Refraining from female touch,
grinding teeth in carnal lust,
wanting what I cannot have…
Abstinence, my unseen foe,
my self-inflicted torment…
Its tearing me up inside,
rising the demon in me…

Such gluttony he brings me,
Craving flesh… to touch… to taste…
To hold… to have… to indulge…
I restrain him, he bites back…
His appetite grows stronger,
filling my mind with dark thoughts,
taunting me to act on them…

'No… I will not appease you…
Do you hear me? Never…'
His rage resounds to my core
I clench my hands to my head,
Temples pounding through fingers…
'Restrain… Restrain…' Tasting blood…
I bit my lip… It tastes good…

I felt pain… And… I liked it…
He laughs, drawing me to him
'Are we really so unlike?
Do you not feel it in you?
We are cut from the same cloth,
you and I, can you feel it?
We have so much work to do'

I shake, he terrifies me
and worse still, he may be right…
I try to suppress his voice,
but these urges… this blood lust…
It fills my mind… Such dark thoughts…
So all consuming… Help me…
I don't want to be evil…

My temperance, my demon,
Suppressing my desires
in exchange for craving flesh…
Please? This is not who I am…
Mincemeat, blue steak… not enough…
I cut myself to sustain,
never sating me… Need more!!!

Doorbell… Young girl from Greenpeace…
Please, come on in, my dear…
She kicks, she claws, she is lost…
Throat slit, pumping blood, wide eyes…
I gasp in sanguine rapture,
Smear her blood on my skin…
Devour her with relish

Pride in temperance, guilt in my gluttony…

*(7 form: 7 verses each with 7 lines each with 7 syllables
with a last line of 7 words)
I created this form for a contest on Allpoetry.com

Someone Please Kill Me

Taking you to terror true,
unconscious from the street.
Keep you doped and tightly roped,
become my carnal treat.
Whimpered plea, 'Please don't hurt me'
I tell you, 'It's alright.'
I tape your mouth and journey south,
And consummate the night.

Grinding hips and fastened lips,
and grasping lady lumps.
Sawing limbs, while singing hymns,
as morphine numbs your stumps.
Flaying skin for what's within,
while keeping you alive.
I decree in blood-soaked glee,
'You'll live but won't survive.'

Carving flesh, so warm and fresh,
with herbs atop my shelf.
Roasting meat, so soft and sweet,
I feed you to yourself.
'Just stay calm, my lucky charm,
I do not wish you pain.
I have to feed this savage need
that's driving me insane.

No more sorrow, come tomorrow,
for you will cease to be.
I know its wrong, but oh so strong,
it haunts and tortures me.'
And so comes death, your final breath
as life fades from your eyes.
Left alone, my monster grown
becomes what I despise.

Please forgive this life I live,
for I have no control.
In too deep and losing sleep
as demons take their toll.
End me please, this sick disease,
just warps and twists my mind.
Make me stop, in death I'll drop
and leave this fiend behind.

Someone please kill me…

Ascending Contemplation

I wait in the shadows,
my life-blood pounding
through my temples
as I peak on the rush
of adrenaline
that surges
through my veins...

I wait, as cramps
start to seize
my limbs in my
motionless state...
I hear footsteps,
tip- tapping
towards me...

Heels on concrete,
if I'm not
very much mistaken...
I hate the sound
of heels on concrete...
Could it be?
Have I found tonight's prey?

Clipety clop, clipety clop,
footsteps louder,
prey is nearer...
Clipety clop, clipety clop,
mind is focused,
thoughts are clearer...

A veil of red
falls over my eyes
as the focus
of my bloodlust
steps into
my line of sight...

My heart hammers
against my ribcage
as I fantasize
the many ways
to extinguish
a single life...

Saliva dribbles
down my chin
and I think
I just had
a mini orgasm...

It's not so much
the act
as the symbolism
it represents...
I think of how easy
it is to snuff
out a candle,
thus outing
the passionate flame
that made it special...

In essence,
wiping out
the endless possibilities
that this soul
might achieve...

Oh, the power!
Oh, the glorious power...
that resides
in these...
my hands...

As tonight's prey
passes me by,
my heartbeat
quickly resumes
back to its regular pace
and I release
the breath
that I didn't realize
I was holding...

I step out
from the shadows
and make
my way home....
I am no killer,
at least
not tonight...

The cravings
are strong,
but I am stronger.
I need to deal
with these cravings.
Do I appease them?
Or do I suppress them?

I guess only time will tell...